The
HERITAGE KEEPER

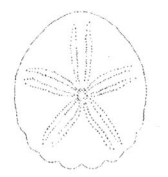

THE
HERITAGE KEEPER

by Jacqueline Leigh

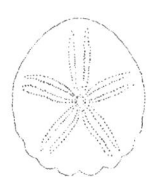

Copyright © 2016 by Jacqueline Leigh. All rights reserved.

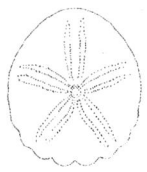

On the
coast of West Africa
in the late 1830s

CHAPTER 1
27th December 1838
Yagoi, on the Jong River

"Fima, you're in charge now."

Mama had started walking down the road. Only her eyes turned sideways toward Fima, but Fima wasn't paying attention. Their nearly hairless puppy, Laneh, was nudging her ankle. He had brought back the dirt-smeared gut of the orange she had just sucked dry and tossed into the tea bush. She scratched his ear and straightened up, turning back to her mother. Mama Boi looked top-heavy, not only from the wide bundle on her head but because her load was crowned with two new hoes for Grandma Karfua.

"You know that I am only leaving this morning because I have to help Grandma."

They had discussed this over and over. Her mother had never left for the village

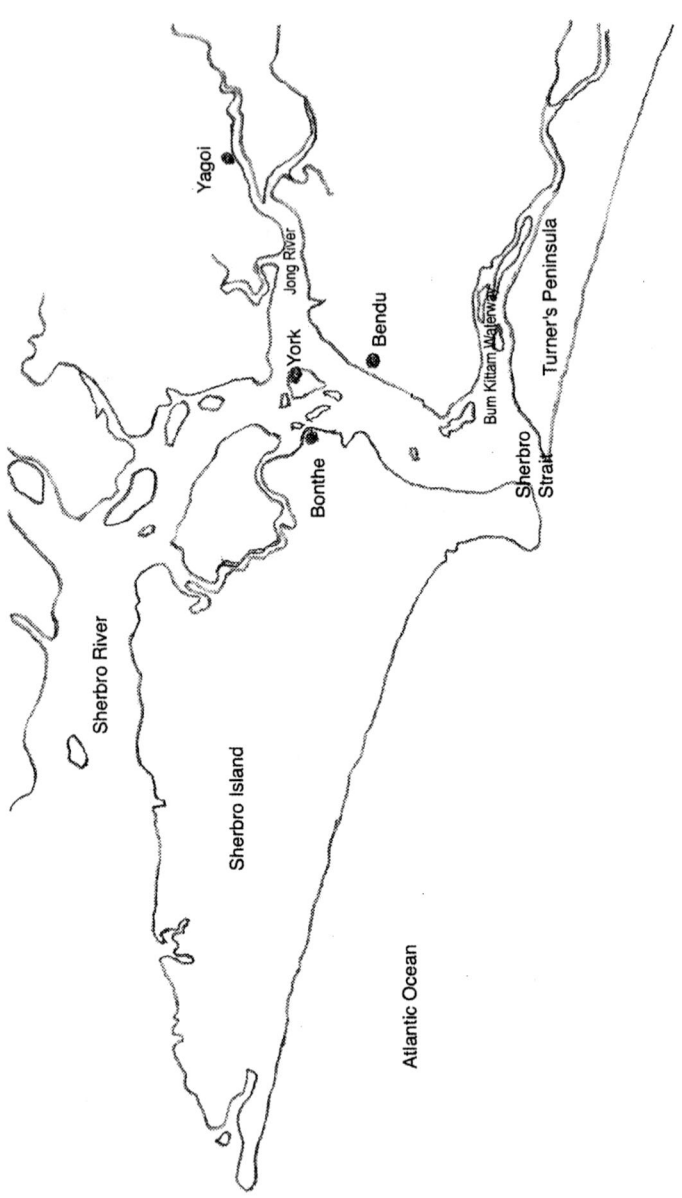

before without waiting for Fima's grandmother to arrive in Yagoi to stay during her absence. This time, Grandma couldn't come. She had injured her leg and not only could not travel, but could not carry on with her work in the village.

"Make sure you deliver all 200 bushels of rice to Banna the Trader today before you set up the stall in the market!" Mama said sternly. "And don't forget: the shipment for Gallinas is due at the waterway by Friday. Don't worry about the Freetown shipment: I'll take care of it when I come."

"I know, Mama," she had said. "I know! You still see me like a child. Have faith in me!"

Their neighbour appeared in her doorway. "Mama Boi, you're travelling? Greet them all for me!"

"I will!" her mother replied, waving. Then she turned back to Fima.

But said nothing. She just stood there looking at her. Fima waited. Mama seemed to be trying to decide something.

Finally, Mama untied her *kotoku*—the knot tying her *lappa*, or skirt-cloth, at her waist. Carefully, she took out the small reddish-brown bundle that she always carried there in addition to her money. "To show you that what you are saying is not true . . .that I do have faith in you, . . . I want you to keep this for me. I don't want to lose it on the trip." Fima stepped back, her eyes wide. Her mother shook her downward-turned fist again, insistently, urging her to take it.

Fima put out her palm, and the object dropped into it. It seemed strange that she had never seen it before! The little leather package was cross-bound with narrow leather straps. She was tempted to smell it, but she didn't. Everyone made fun of the way that she had never grown out of the need to know how things smelled. She closed her other hand over it.

Fima raised her *docket* and tied the bundle tightly inside her own *kotoku*. She pulled her *docket* back down over it again very firmly. She looked down and patted it to check that it was covered. Straightening up, she looked at the ground. Her body felt awkward, as if she should look or stand in a different way now that she carried a woman's burden.

Her mother started to talk but Fima interrupted her. "Mama, you do not have to say it again. You have told me so many times: Great-Grandma Fima had to leave when Grandma Karfua was still a baby, so she gave the bundle to a friend to keep until Grandma Karfua grew up. And then Grandma Karfua kept it until you were old enough, and then she gave it to you. We must never lose it or open it. If it is ever opened, something very bad will happen that could destroy us. Stop worrying! I understand. Thank you for trusting me. I will keep it safe."

She touched her *kotoku* again; it had no money in it, but the small bundle weighed more than she had thought it would. *Strange that it has weight,* she thought.

Mama had smiled at her and said, "'God is our refuge and strength'," and Fima had answered as she did every morning during their prayers, "'a very present help in trouble'."

And then Mama had turned away. A breeze had risen suddenly. She had adjusted her neck and shoulders in a snakelike movement to keep her load from capsizing. Then she had set off on the two-day walking journey to their village, Mengbinteh.

"Greet Papa for me," Fima had called after her. "And tell Grandma not to worry. God will mend her leg. You packed the rope I made for her fishing nets, didn't you?" Her mother waved from a distance. "Mama, when are you going to take me to the village?"

Her mother had waved again, without turning. Fima had known there would be no answer. Her mother had always said that going to Mengbinteh was not safe for Fima. Bad people live there, she would say. They could harm her. Who, or why, Fima didn't know. She did not actually give it much thought. She had spent most of her life here at the mouth of the Jong River, near where it emptied into the Sherbro River and went on out the Strait into the sea. So she was not surprised when her mother had simply continued on her way.

That was this morning. Now, inside their mud-block and palm-thatch warehouse, she boosted the last bushel-bag of rice onto the porter's shoulders. He turned toward the river where Kai was waiting with the rest of the load at the canoe landing. Dependable Kai, so smart in his gold-embroidered light blue long-sleeved shirt and trousers this morning! He must really care for her, if he had offered his canoe when he could be at work earning money! It certainly made the trip to Banna's much easier.

Her mother had been worried about how

she would go. "Don't come home alone with the payment!" she had warned. "Go with one of the porters—Toby is the most dependable—and make sure he comes back with you." Toby was a Kruman, one of the hundreds of itinerant porters along the coast who carried loads for a fee.

But after she left, Kai had come by. He did not normally run the Yagoi-York Island route. Usually he worked the Bum-Kittam waterway along Turner's Peninsula, carrying rice from the Sherbro to the busy Gallinas port where there were thousands of slaves in barracoons to feed and slave vessels needing provisions. Gallinas seemed to have an endless demand for rice, everyone in Sherbro commented. No one complained, of course. It was lucky for the Sherbro hinterland that the soil in Gallinas was not fertile enough to supply their needs.

But this morning, Kai had appeared. It would be a slow morning on the waterway, he had said, so he was available to help take her loads to Banna the Trader at York Island. *If Mama had been here*, Fima thought, *she would have announced, "Fima, your suitor is here."* It always embarrassed her when her mother called him that and she would look around hoping that no one had heard.

CHAPTER 2
Two months earlier
In a barracoon in the Sherbro River

Sau
It happened during rice planting, just before the rains.

I know, I have no one to blame. I am my own worst enemy. Everyone says so. Too bold. Too independent. But you must understand: I was about to be married, and our mother is a member of The Circle. So people had started expecting more of me. All we were trying to do (my identical twin Jina and I) was to persuade the women to change their planting methods a little, to get more out of the land.

Well, the village chief didn't like it. He sold me to a slave trader that came through the village. What a shock!

I was still in shock as we set off walking.

Jina was in the crowd, watching as we left. She had tried to tell the chief to sell her, too, but I stopped her by reminding her of all the ways our family needed her.

She reached out her arm and we touched our upright palms, whispering "Jina for Sau . . . Sau for Jina" just as we have done since we were small to promise that we would always support each other, whatever life brought. And then we were gone off down the path.

I have never walked so far. We passed village after village picking up more and more people on the way. The only thing we ate was a small amount of dried rice. The rains were still coming then. We passed Koribundu in a heavy storm. I cannot say how many days, or how many miles we walked, slipping and falling in the deep mud with that rough rope chafing our necks before we reached this barracoon where they locked us in.

They say this is Sherbro where we are now. I do not know. All we can see is bush. You know those pens where they keep goats? That's what barracoons look like, but they're closed over the top and they keep you chained up. Not everyone can sit at one time. And we have no clothes! No one here even knows my name. They give us rice and water. If the water they give us is the same as everyone drinks in this place, I am sorry for them. How lucky our village is to have such good wells and springs!

Imagine, Jina, spending the night outside during this time when the rains come at night, those frightening gales followed by lightning and thunder! And they keep flogging us. . . . They flick their whips and dole out lashes for no reason. Just to control us, I think. The men have come to just expect it, and hardly cry out any more.

Jina, don't follow me here!

All I was trying to do was to tell people that what the chief was saying wasn't true. Our planting ideas are not new. They are very old. They weren't brought from the outside world as he said, but from right within our people. I thought he didn't know, and I thought he would want to learn.

We know this story to be true:

Many generations ago, five villages in our area were closer than they are today. They were nearby, because they did not have to hide from the world like we do today to continue our traditions. They also cooperated more. Farm planting teams and harvesting teams came from all five of the villages. Ceremonies and feasts did not happen in just one village at a time, but in all at once.

Each village had its own water wells, but the five also shared a spring. It was a special spring, sacred to all of the villagers. They did not use it casually or freely. Five women—one from each village—met at the spring regularly to maintain it and to collect water from it for ceremonies. They would linger there. True, they were not young women, but they did not linger only to rest. They listened to the flow rise through the rocks. One would begin to talk. She wished she could re-route all the irrigation channels, or re-apportion the land. The others answered. One would re-organize farmworkers if she too had the power. And the others answered. Another would plant and harvest more often. And the others answered. Their talk came from far away, and their talk was deep because of the long years of knowing and work they brought with them.

These women were called The Circle. When they returned home, their ideas passed onto their sisters and daughters until all the women in all five of the villages were part of the discussion.

One day when The Circle arrived at the spring, they found, laid out on the rock before them, five small sand-dollar fossils, each no bigger than a groundnut.

They wondered at the sand dollars, away from the seashore as they were, arrayed neatly in a circle at the sacred spring. They were grainy to the touch, light as clouds, and marked like flowers with five fine petals front and back. Surely they were signs from a greater power.

And it is from these fossils that The Circle's power began: from the signs that were given to our ancestors, the guardians of the spring. The women returned to their villages with their fossils. Everyone was astonished at the news. Everyone celebrated and stood in awe at what had come to be.

But then things began to happen to the elder women in the villages. Objects went missing, and they were blamed. Work they had done was said to have been done by others.. Some reported that they had defied elders when they had not spoken at all. So they were traded off, sold away. I don't mean they went to the next village, or the next district. They disappeared altogether. They never came back. They were gone forever.

And when we asked for the women of The Circle, we found they had all disappeared! Killed? Sold? Traded? Kidnapped? There was no trace of them. And no trace of their sand-dollar fossils.

But we the women had heard The Voice. We implemented their ideas. Since then we have not stopped implementing them. Whenever we can, we in The Circle try new ways to increase the output of our farms. My mother's generation has worked hard at this. Her groundnuts paid for all our tuitions. We will do the same for our children.

In our village, I thought the men were not even noticing us. Foolishly, I began explaining. At first I thought the elders were listening to me but then I realised that they had known the whole story and all our plans all along, and had only been pretending not to know. What is important to them is that the farmland is community land. I think they feared that we would ask for more recognition. Or more land to farm. Or that we would say the land belonged to us and take power that does not belong to us.

When the chief sold me, my mother said only one thing to me. She said, "Sau, I have always told you: some things should not be said." I felt bad about that. I suppose I thought she would support me. I know she wishes I were more courteous, like Jina. But I don't don't blame Mama. I am sure she has never seen a barracoon. She can't have known that I would be chained like this, for months. That we try to sing, but our songs become moans. That many here are losing hope.

And Jina. I know her bowels cry out with my hunger. She must wince at every lash of the whip. I know she shivers when the night winds blow through this pen. I only pray that she will not try to find me . . .

CHAPTER 3
27th December 1838
Yagoi

Fima had no doubt that she could get along fine by herself. Her mother would be proud of her when she returned. She had been working—pushing, pulling, lifting half-bushels of rice—all day. Now that this was the last load, she prepared to board the canoe, too.

She checked the lower shelf of the *banda*, or rack, where their fish was slowly drying. She moved the snapper to the upper shelf, further from the heat, and covered them with leaves, leaving the larger sections of fish where they were. She set two more pieces of firewood from the pile of red mangrove to dry at the edge of the coals.

She crossed over to their outdoor kitchen, walking past one of the sides where the pillowed elephant grass was trimmed to about a foot above the ground, to enter at the open end. She took her pot of cooked rice off the firestones. Half the entrance had been blocked with woven palm fronds to protect the hearth from the wind. It was in that corner that she tucked her rice now. She would cook the sauce this afternoon. Potato leaves, she thought. Her mother didn't like it so Fima only made it when she was away.

In the house, she changed to a clean *docket* and *lappa*, carefully securing the leather bundle in her *kotoku* as she had seen her mother do so many times. Approaching the door to leave, her eyes fell on the heavy round wooden pestle leaning against the door hinges. She smiled, remembering her grandmother's admonition: "We always say to keep a pestle behind the door: you never know when your neighbour will suddenly go off his head." Shaking her head at Grandma's traditional ways, she locked the door on her way out and turned down to the landing.

"This rice must be for the *Violante*," Kai called out to her as she began descending along the clump of bamboo toward the water's edge. "Have you seen her—that green and white schooner in the Strait? Just off York Island? She must be 80 tons or so. They loaded her this morning." Fima started down to the water. "What a racket! I don't know who is noisier when they're loading, the slaves or the traders!" he said. "The traders are making as much noise as they can with their whips to get them to get into the boats, and the slaves are moaning and crying, and the traders are cursing them and their chains are rattling. . . . There were lots of children this time so they were screaming, too. The captains are getting smart now, buying mostly children. They cost less and you get more years of work out of them.

"Anyway, whatever they pay here for slaves, the traders sell them for four times as much in Cuba." Kai moved to another seat to make way for the next rice bag. "Fima, you won't believe how the owners live over in Cuba."

"Mmm," Fima was watching where she was stepping, and only half listening. She was holding Laneh in the crook of one arm. Her foot skidded on the rubble. A swirl of wind brought a loud clacking and swishing in the bamboo next to her and blew dust into her face. She stopped to wipe it out of her eyes. The harmattan had its disadvantages, there was no doubt about that, but it was her season. It marked the time of her birth, so each year it meant that she was one year older.

"Do you want me to keep the dog for you?" Toby asked Fima, waiting at the bow to shove them off. Fima smiled at him knowing Laneh would be safe with him. But she knew also that Toby would spend the day trying to get work along the shore and that he would have no place to keep a puppy.

"Yes, take it," Kai answered, with a wave of his hand. "Dogs aren't suited for canoes."

Fima looked down at him disdainfully over her shoulder. "Laneh is coming with us," she stated, and with that, she climbed in.

Kai looked at her but did not reply. He and his apprentice picked up their paddles and pushed against the mangrove while Toby gave them a shove from shore, his feet sunk well into the mud. Once they had left him behind and joined the current, they stayed close to the mangrove bank.

Kai resumed talking. "As I was saying, Fima, those owners live like kings. Wait till I have my own vessel. My schooner will slice into the wind as clean as a knife. If I can get a 100-ton I can take up to 300 slaves at a time. It's money that makes the world go round, you know—and I am going to be rich!"

Fima was not paying much attention. Kai had told her this many times before. She was watching the path of sparkling water the canoe carved along its side as it passed along the river. She was tempted to run her fingers through the spray but imagined a crocodile's open mouth full of teeth and kept her hands close.

"God will help you succeed," she said, absent-mindedly.

"You and I, we'll run the business from both sides. My vessels will buy rice only from your mother at the shop here. We can direct everything from our mansion in Cuba!"

This was a banter they had engaged in many times. "Me in Cuba?" she scoffed, looking sideways at him. "What would I want to do in Cuba? I have told you, Kai, I'm going to have my own shop. I will be independent. I won't need a partner. I'll have wagons and carts so I will hardly even need porters. Did you know there used to be two- and four-wheeled carts here? I don't know what happened to them."

"Well, I do: it's the bad roads. Do you see any road here good enough for wheels, especially when the rains have gutted it out? And which animal do you imagine is going to pull your carts?" He leant forward suddenly.

"Fima, get that dog of yours off my boot!" He swatted at the dog but Laneh jumped out of his reach.

Laneh had dragged a boot out from under the bow deck with his teeth, and dropped it at Fima's feet. Fima had seen them before: magnificent boots Kai had received from a Spanish trader as payment for ferrying services. He took great pride in owning them but she had never seen him wear them. Laneh wagged his curved long tail as he looked at her, panting expectantly. She ran her fingers through his tail, a white fly whisk performing a backbend on his back.

Kai continued, "If you had a cart, you'd still have to call a porter to pull or push it." He laughed. "And he'd rather carry the cart on his head than push it! In Cuba, you know, I'll have a carriage. We'll ride around just for pleasure."

She did not reply. They had reached the trader's dock at York Island. Kai's apprentice was helping Banna's porters secure the canoe so they could offload the rice. Kai stayed seated in the stern with Fima.

It was Fima's turn to get out, but Kai put

a hand on her arm, stalling her. Her heart jumped. *Was he waiting for the porters to go?* She smiled to herself. *Maybe he wanted to kiss her. Maybe he had something to tell her that he didn't want the others to hear . . . ?*

But when the last porter had disappeared up over the bank, Kai took his hand away. He picked up his paddle. *Why had he held her back? Had he changed his mind?*

His apprentice re-appeared. "Yes, well, that's the last of the load," Kai said. "So Fima, you can return home on your own, right?" Fima looked at him in surprise. Surely he would want to see her safely back home. Seeing her look, he said, "Did you expect me to spend the whole day not making money?"

Fima felt foolish. Her stomach tightened. In her mind, she could hear her mother saying *"Don't come home alone with the payment!"* very clearly this morning. She wished she had thought to ask Toby to meet her at Banna's shop, just to be sure she had someone to go home with. She had nothing with her that she could exchange for the canoe trip back.

But once she had collected the payment from Banna she would have money. She suddenly grew impatient with herself. Is this how an independent trader would behave? She didn't need Kai, or anyone else. She could do this on her own. Standing up with her puppy, she tossed her head like a duster erasing finished work from a chalkboard and said, "Of course I'll be fine! And you can expect our rice for Gallinas at the waterway on Friday."

And she marched up the dirt steps to Banna the Trader's without looking back.

CHAPTER 4
York Island

Banna—a fair-skinned, round-bellied man with a pointed grey-and-black beard—was alone in his shop behind the counter drinking coffee. Fima greeted him but he couldn't have heard her because as soon as they entered, Laneh's soft growl had escalated into barking. He jumped to the floor barking at Banna, stepping back, and then barking again. He kept moving out of her reach while she tried to quiet him. He was everywhere, like oranges spilling out of a capsized bushel basket.

"Laneh, what is the matter with you?" she asked in a frustrated voice.

"Fima, good morning." She had never seen Banna without his grey captain's cap, and he had it on today. "Captain Marcolino from the *Violante* is in a hurry to clear the river but he refused to pay me until he received the entire order. He sent his longboat. It's right here at the wharf waiting for you."

He stood up and called the porters waiting outside. "This is the last of the shipment for the *Violante*," he said to them. "Take it down to the longboat. You will see it waiting at the wharf."

Then he turned to Fima. "Here . . . (he wrote quickly on a piece of paper) . . .you can go out with them and hand this to the captain. He'll pay you directly."

She took the paper but looked at him doubtfully.

"Look, there it is," pointed Banna, seeing her hesitation. "Do you see that green and white schooner? It's only 50 yards out. Just follow the porters. Why not leave the dog here? You won't be needing it."

"Not be needing him? Why?" The dog's heart was still beating fast, and she was trying to calm him.

"I meant, won't he be in your way?" He smiled and shrugged. "Do as you like. But he will be safe here," he said pointing behind the counter, "and you can collect him on your way back." Fima looked at Laneh. He had big brown eyes, full of faith—full of *laneh*. He was growling when she handed him over and watched as Banna put him on the floor behind the counter, but he went because he trusted her, Fima thought.

The three men in the longboat looked up at them as Fima and the porters approached. They all looked Spanish or Portuguese, as did most of the slave traders who came to Sherbro. By the time they finished loading the rice, it had filled the longboat. A heavy-set man with a mass of curly hair helped her in and she sat down near him on top of the rice.

"Hey, Sebastian!" an old man sitting in the bow called out as soon as he reached out to help her. "You have new wife? You married yesterday?" They all burst out laughing.

The *Violante* looked much larger when they reached next to it and her eyes rose from the water level to the top of the sails. Sebastian reached out and grasped the rope ladder slapping against the vessel, to keep the boat steady for her. She took hold and began the climb up, thanking Banna with each step for keeping Laneh.

At the top a very dirty, hairy hand reached out for her. She put her hand out, and he seized it and pulled her over the rail. Once on her feet, she pulled her hand quickly away from the man and stepped back. She wondered if she had been rude.

Would he have noticed that she was repelled by him? He stood with his legs apart like she had seen a monkey do when it was threatening to attack. Taking care not to meet his eyes, she asked for Captain Marcolino. Without moving the rest of his body, he pointed with his chin toward an open door behind her.

She saw a slim, neatly bearded uniformed officer wearing wire spectacles when she peeked in. He was sitting at a desk, writing in a ledger. "Good evening, Mr. Captain, sir. I have brought the last of the rice. They are loading it now. Mr. Banna sent you this note." The man didn't move, so she extended her hand so he could see that she was holding something. She was still standing at the door. Then he turned slowly to look at her, and wordlessly, held out his hand. *If this captain is in a hurry,* she thought*, he must be a chameleon*! But he had held out his hand, so she approached.

Just as she was taking a third step from the door, bang! It slammed behind her. A cold, heavy metal hit her throat and circled her neck. It clamped shut. The collar weighed her down sideways. She grasped at it with both hands.

"Wha . . . what are you doing?" she said

hoarsely. The collar was thick and rough, with a short rod attached to it by round links. Her fingers moved up the rod. She felt ragged nails and a hairy hand and snatched her hand away.

She was yanked backwards and fell against someone. She hung, half standing, half sitting, suspended by the collar around her neck. The man turned her to face a dark corner of the room. "Cargo finish, Señor Barba," he said in a rough voice.

A man stepped forward just then out of the shadows. He wore an open-necked, white, long-sleeved embroidered shirt. He had a bristly grey moustache and grey and black hair parted well over to one side. His smile showed all his teeth and nearly closed his eyes. He looked Fima up and down as if he were buying her instead of her rice. Slowly, he brought a curved pipe up to his mouth.

"Bueno, Gregorio," he said, with his teeth clenched on his pipe. Something was strange about the man's teeth. They were too pearly, like fish scales. "She's a strong one. She'll bring a good price."

"What? No!" Fima croaked, twisting her head toward the captain. "Ask the captain! It's a mistake! I'm not a slave!" She tried to stand up but she could not reach the floor to push herself. The man called Gregorio jerked her up. She elbowed him hard in the ribs and aimed a kick where she thought his knee would be. She was glad to hear a grunt of pain.

The man called Barba chuckled. "This one looks like she is too much for you, Gregorio! Maybe I should call someone who knows how to control a woman?"

"Let me go! I am a trader! Ask the captain! I came for my mother's money! Look!" She held up her hand to show the note again but it was no longer there. The collar prevented her from looking down onto the floor to see where it had fallen. She twisted her head hard to look back at the captain and a rough spur on the iron cut into the flesh under her jaw. She winced and touched it with her palm.

Her hand came away smeared with bright blood. But in that quick turn, she had caught sight of the captain. He was no longer at the desk. He was standing with his back towards them, looking out the window. She wondered if he might be deaf. He looked as if he had no idea what was going on.

The husky sailor called Gregorio had opened the door. With the rod, he pushed her out onto the deck. She kicked him in the leg again and just then, the vessel tipped. When the rod flopped against her back she knew he had lost hold of her.

She ran toward the gunwale looking for footholds she could use to climb onto the ladder. When she had straddled the railing, what she saw astonished her. On shore she could clearly see Banna in front of his shop, and . . . with him, . . . Kai? Was that Kai in his light blue clothes? But hadn't Kai returned to work already? Why was he at the shop?

"Kai! Mr. Banna! Help!" she screamed at them, "Help me!" But the wind wrapped itself around her cries as they left her tongue, and flew with them out to sea.

She was almost onto the ladder when the vessel tipped back seaward and Gregorio pulled her off the railing. His arm passed in front of her face to grasp the iron rod, and she bit into the muscle of his forearm. Roaring in anger, he snatched his hand back and swung his other elbow into her back, knocking her to the deck.

Then he pulled her to her feet and yanked at her clothes. "Off!" With his free left hand he tore her *docket* open and threw it. It was bright red! Fima stared at it until she realised her cut was still bleeding. He ripped her string of waist beads and they rolled everywhere. A dagger appeared, and he slashed open her *kotoku*.

Fima bent over to try to hold onto her *lappa*. Just in time, her palm was open when something small and gold dropped into it. She tossed it into her mouth and forced it—full of corners and tasting metallic—under her tongue so she wouldn't swallow it. Then she watched, stunned, as the leather bits of the bundle, given legs by the wind, scampered like small crabs across the deck of the vessel. Two water birds flew across the deck plucking them up in their beaks. The rest passed under the railing and tumbled to the sea below.

The bundle! Her mother's bundle had opened! The thing that was never to be! How could she, Fima, do what all her ancestors had warned their children against? No one before her had failed to uphold the tradition. Her heart was beating like a fast drum. Everything became dim and Fima staggered. Gregorio pulled her up and kept tearing at her *lappa*.

Fima no longer cared. She felt nothing. When he gave it a hard jerk, she let the cloth fall away, and fainted.

Fima awoke to sharp pain. Gregorio was flicking at her with a whip. He pointed to a hole in the deck. The hinged door was swung open. A dank smell rose to her nose. An unhappy smell. She squinted inside but all she could see were two rungs of a ladder.

"Pa' abajo!" He gave her a shove. "Down!"

He followed her into the dark, pulling the door down after them. It was not a solid door. It was criss-crossed with wooden and iron bars.

He did not let go of the rod, and with each step he took he jerked her neck. It got hotter and hotter and harder to breathe. They reached another deck and walked a short way. From the light that came through the hatch, she could see hundreds of feet, bound together in irons. They went down another ladder into almost complete darkness. There were women's voices here, and the voices of children. They moved slowly down the shelf along the wall. All the women's ankles were manacled to the board, and their heads at the hull wall.

The man called Gregorio unclamped her neck and pushed her onto the shelf next to another woman.

At that moment, on the shelf on her

knees, facing the side of the vessel, she spat out the flat squarish gold piece that her tongue had protected. There in front of her nose in the dark, she could just make out a knot in the hull. Over it, there was a crack. She pushed the piece hard into the crack, and it fit! It fit all the way in!

"Ay!" Fima's chin hit against the shelf hard as Gregorio yanked her ankles to flatten her on the board. When he flipped her to her back her head hit the shelf overhead. She kicked and her toes caught his chest, unbalancing him. He nearly fell.

Righting himself, he snarled at her, "You finish!" He took the double handcuffs attached to the girl next to her and tried to close the second cuff around her wrist. It was too small so he raised his iron rod high in the air to strike the cuff and force it to close. Fima watched the rod begin to descend and tried to move her hand, but she couldn't. When it hit, she screamed. Gregorio let out a great, harsh laugh. Then he pulled her right ankle, and she heard another cuff lock.

"Me boss!" he said to her, his right thumb pointing to his chest. And he sneered, showing only one side of his teeth. As he turned to go, the ship heeled. Fima and the girl were pushed by the force over the rough board toward the wall of the vessel. The manacles pulled on her wrist and ankle, and she winced.

Fima lay thinking for a long time about what had happened and how she had come to be where she was. *If only she had brought Laneh onto the schooner,* she thought, *he would have taken a good bite out of that man's leg. He would have taught him a lesson!* But then thinking what Gregorio might have done in revenge, she was glad she had left him behind.

Just before closing her eyes, she said to herself, *Where is the pestle now, Grandma, now that my whole world has gone off its head?*

CHAPTER 5
Hours later
On the Violante in the Sherbro River

Fima opened her eyes, and panicked. *Boxed up, buried. Breathe, Fima, breathe!*

She imagined her mother's broad smile, the same strong smile she gave her as she was standing in the road. *God is our refuge and strength.*

The waves slapped against the side of the vessel. Her wrist hurt. She looked down at her hand on the cuff, and her eyes passed to the other cuff and up the very bony arm of the woman next to her. The person was looking at her. Her face was like a skeleton's. It was only after Fima looked carefully at her that she decided she must be alive. And she must be about her own age. Someone ought to speak, she thought.

"I'm not supposed to be here," Fima said quickly. "They made a mistake. I'm not like the rest of you. I'm not a slave."

The girl sighed and looked up and down Fima's naked body, and said, "Well, don't worry, my girl, no one will know. You fit in just fine." And she chuckled, and the woman on the other side of Fima made a noise like a half cough. As if she had forgotten how to laugh.

Fima's face grew hot with shame. Just trying to turn away pulled on her sore hand and made her jaw hurt. She was glad for the darkness and closed her eyes. How would she ever prove to anyone who she was? Maybe Kai was asking for her. Was that why he was at Banna's? Surely he would come and take her home!

And then she remembered the packet her mother had given her. She stiffened. Her eyes flew open.

What if this isn't a mistake? Maybe this is intended for me. When Mama handed over the bundle she did not know that it was my fate to release the evil. Is this the plan for my life? They say we should accept our destiny. If this is how our family will end, there is nothing that can be done about it. She felt too empty to cry.

Lying there silent, she gradually heard what the people around her were saying. *Was that praying? Did slaves pray,* she wondered? She had never met a slave before. A man began singing. Sadly, softly. Others joined in. She fell asleep.

When Fima awoke, her head was higher than her feet. The vessel was leaning. It was still dark. She couldn't tell if it was night or day. They tipped back, and she was level again. The water swished loudly against the outside of the hull. It must be rushing past. They must have left the Strait. Were they in the ocean?

She touched her right hand. It was puffy. Strangely, she could not even feel it.

"How is your neck? It hurts, doesn't it?" The girl's voice was softer now. "If I were at home in my village, I know what I would put on it."

"Thanks to God, I can bear it. What is your name?" Fima asked her.

"I'm Sau."

"You have a twin name. Is your twin here—your Jina? Are you both slaves?"

"I wasn't a slave. You're not the only one here who wasn't a slave. Many of us were not. It was our village chief who sold me."

"Why?"

She paused, and then asked, "Which village are you from? Are you a village girl?"

When Fima explained that she knew very little about their village, Sau told her about the people she had talked to in the barracoon. Some had been traded because they showed disrespect. Some had been provoked into a conflict, and were taken prisoner.

"Do you know about The Circle?" When Fima said no, Sau explained the story of how she, herself, had been traded for encouraging the villagers to understand the ideas of The Circle, and how The Circle began.

"The chief probably does not know that the women's ideas came from the old ones. Does he know what happened at the spring?" said Fima.

"He knows. Everyone knows." Sau was quiet for a bit. Then she said, "Fima, what do you think will happen to us? Some say they are going to eat us. I don't think so, do you? While we were walking, the only thing we ate was dried rice and in the barracoon all they gave us was plain rice and water. If they were going to eat us, wouldn't they be giving us good food so we would get fat?"

"My friend told me that these people don't do anything to slaves except sell them. They are doing this for money, to get rich. He said this vessel takes slaves to Cuba to sell."

"Cuba? Where is that? Is it far?"

"I don't know. I didn't think I would ever be going there." What a fool she was to have joked with Kai about Cuba!

Her hand began to hurt again. The hull creaked. The water rushing past sounded deep and frightening and the rocking was making her sick. She could hear people vomiting. The sour odour of the hold had grown worse. Of course! There was nowhere to vomit or toilet except right where they lay.

Fima dozed off, but this time, she dreamed. Kai—a plump Kai with fat cheeks, in a shiny caftan—was lying on their verandah in Cuba on red and gold cushions, sipping a drink. She was beside him. They were waiting for their slaver to arrive. She stood up in a sparkling gown and pointed with a bejewelled forefinger toward their vessel on the horizon.

The water was very blue in the sunshine.

Then a howling began to rise from deep inside the vessel. It grew louder and louder and took shape. Spectres grunted and shuddered out through every opening and rose grey and grasping into the air, smelling like the rotten carcasses of rats. They spewed over the water and as the slaver came near, she could see ghosts inside, writhing and moaning.

And she was one of them! She was inside the slaver with them. She was chained hand and foot, her hair matted and her face bruised. She turned toward the person she was chained to and the face became her mother's face. It was her mother lying there dead next to her, decaying, with hollow eyes and no teeth.

Fima awoke shaking her head wildly and shouting, "No! No!" pushing and jerking Sau up to a sitting position.

"Ay! Ay!" Sau cried. "What's happening? Calm down!" Fima could feel the warmth from Sau's body, and her closeness. How she missed her puppy! She love hugging his warm body and looking into his soft brown eyes!

Then to her amazement she noticed she was gulping air like a little child who has spent herself crying. Every time she gasped, one of the woman spoke.

"Take heart, child."

"Don't be afraid, God is with us."

"We will survive, my daughter." She could not see them but they sounded like real women—like her mother and her grandmother, not like slaves. Slowly, she lay back down, and began to breathe more slowly. The women asked if she had quieted down, and Sau told them she had. Fima did not answer. She could stay independent in the dark.

She had so many questions. Why hadn't Kai waited for her? And Toby. Would he stop by for a job and notice that she had not returned home? Maybe he would just look elsewhere, knowing there would be less work with her mother away. Where would Laneh be? What would happen to him? And Mama—she was so far away.

CHAPTER 6
28th December 1838
Back in Yagoi

Toby was worried. The day before, he had expected that Fima would have returned quickly. All she had to do was deliver her bags of rice, collect the money and turn back with Kai. She had set aside the rice she wanted to take to the market to sell and she would need a porter to help with that.

Thinking back on the day, Toby would have made more money if he had followed their canoe to the Strait so he could continue checking with the team leaders for work. That would have been the smart thing to do. Instead he had moved up and down along the Jong so he could stay near the warehouse. He had last checked it at nightfall. Fima had not returned.

This morning, back in the Strait on York Island, he found Banna in his shop sitting sharing a drink with a friend behind the counter.

"Fima? After I paid her, she left. I haven't seen her since. Wasn't it that fellow of hers—Kai—who brought her here?"

"Yes, in his canoe."

Banna looked at his friend, shook his head, took a drink, and chuckled. "And now you tell me she didn't go straight home. Well, are you surprised? That's youth, my man! If your mother's not in town, you have a bit of fun. There's no harm in that, is there?"

Toby admitted that that could've happened. But he did not turn away. He could not really imagine Fima doing such a thing. Especially on the day that her mother had left.

"What's the problem? Has someone made you her guardian?" Banna asked, seeing that Toby seemed reluctant to accept his answer. Banna's question was a mocking one and it had the effect Banna intended. After all, Toby was only a here-and-there porter. Embarrassed, Toby shook his head, stepped back and turned away. Banna was right. What business was it of his?

He spent the day loading and offloading vessels in the Strait, but he wasn't as carefree as usual. Something gnawed at him.

Something Banna had said didn't fit. He couldn't put his finger on it.

Having finished one job, Toby turned south along the edge of a swamp on York Island. In the grasses there he heard a noise. Parting the leaves he was surprised to find a very dirty Laneh. The dog yelped when he reached for him and cringed as if he were afraid of him. Toby picked him up and carried him over to a tree but the dog kept giving small painful cries. He offered his lunch to him in bits which disappeard almost as soon as he had put them down.

As he ate, Toby could see that what had looked like dirt on his hair was actually dried blood. In fact, he was covered with cuts and bruises. What could have happened? Toby couldn't imagine anyone having the power to take him out of Fima's hands. Surely if she had gone off to enjoy herself with Kai, she would have taken her dog.

Toby crossed over to the Bum-Kittam waterway to talk to Kai.

"Kai?" The club-footed boatman shook his head at Toby's question. "I haven't seen Kai here for weeks." He looked over at the boy in the next canoe for confirmation. He shook his head, too.

Toby stared at them, his mouth open. Hadn't Kai said that the reason he had been able to help Fima was because yesterday would be a slow morning on the waterway? He had given the impression that he worked on the Bum-Kittam every day.

An old fisherman sitting on a rock with his net over his knee, misunderstood his surprise. "You're a porter—you know yourself that business here is slow during the dry season when the canoes can't get all the way through to the Gallinas River. The last eight miles you have to do by sea or on foot now." Toby nodded—there was always work for porters when the canoes couldn't get through. "And these boys don't sit still. If they can't be sure of making good money quickly, they would rather move on than pay their dues to the headman to work here. Boatmen always have another plan."

A plan. Suddenly Toby remembered what it was Banna had said that struck him as odd: *If your mother's not in town.* How did Banna know that Fima's mother had travelled? Who would have told him? "Mm-hmm," he said aloud. "Someone with a plan. Someone with a plan."

Toby had no choice but to take Fima's dog home with him. After he had eaten, he sat looking at the sleeping puppy, still curled up next to the door. Suddenly he squinted and leant forward to see better.

A bit of colour seemed fastened between his claws. Drawing it out carefully, he found it was a ragged bit of light blue cotton, the same blue damask he had seen on Kai the day before, embroidered in gold at the bottom of the sleeves and trousers. He closed his eyes, and in his mind he could imagine the whistle of a bamboo cane, and the smack and yelp it caused when it landed on a strong small nearly-hairless puppy that refused to let go or stop growling until he ripped a piece off the bottom edge of his tormenter's trousers.

CHAPTER 7
Early on the same day
Twenty miles out of the Sherbro Strait

KA**BOOM**! BOO-DOO-**BOOM**!
Was the explosion inside or outside? Inside this very hold where they were confined? Children screamed. Everyone shouted. Would they sink? They couldn't swim! These shackles! This was the open ocean! The water devil would take them! Talking of the devil made the children scream louder.

"Heave to!" a speaking-trumpet shouted. Loud thuds like irons clanked against the deck, followed by the rippling of ropes, trampling footsteps, and voices shouting in Spanish. The vessel pitched suddenly, and then seemed to come to a stop.

Soon they heard a pounding, and the commanding sound of disciplined boots, timed footsteps and sharp voices. Before long, the hatch opened. A shaft of light shone down into the hull. Someone gagged. Someone retched. There were sounds of disgust. Men in military hats and blue uniforms peered in at them. When they receeded, others took their places. Then then hatch was closed again.

There was much shouting up on deck. Soon, two military men, with cutlasses and revolvers, climbed down the ladders, clanking into the hold. One was a white man, dressed as a naval officer, and one was an African, in a green uniform. Gregorio and Sebastian came behind them. The white officer spoke in a loud voice.

When he had finished he stepped back saying, "Corporal?" and with the palm of his hand, motioned the officer in the green uniform to step forward to speak.

He greeted everyone and began to explain: They were the crew of the *HMS Brisk*, a cruiser of the British Royal Navy. It was their job to find and capture slave trading vessels, and they had arrested the captain and crew of the *Violante*. The Royal Navy was taking the vessel to Sierra Leone to be tried in the Court of Mixed Commission. When the court had condemned the vessel, all of them would be set free there, in Freetown, where they would be under the protection of the Queen of England. For now, the shackles would be removed from everyone, and they would give each person something to wear.

Those who understood the message began to call out thanks and to pray loudly. As the word spread, more and more throughout the hold shouted out in relief.

The white officer turned to Gregorio and Sebastian. "Release them! These people need air, and water. I want to see them all up on deck. Now! If they can't walk you will help them up the ladder." There was much talking and counting and pointing at everything. The officer wrote things down as they went through the hold handing out a *lappa* for each person and opening all the shackles.

As Gregorio reached to undo Fima's handcuff, he looked into her eyes and very slowly raised his index finger to the left side of his throat and drew it across to the right. Both Fima and Sau, with wide eyes, tried to pull themselves back, away from his sinister threat.

Sensing the odd silence, the Corporal turned toward them. "What's the problem here?" Then he said to the other officer, "Look: the cut on this girl's jaw is septic.

And can you believe the size of the handcuffs they put on these girls? At least that one's wrist is thin, but this one's is cut and swollen. It is probably broken."

"Don't worry," he said to Fima. "You will go to hospital as soon as we land."

Finally they were climbing the ladder. When Fima reached the top deck, she raised her head to the sky and took the deepest breath she could of the early morning air. It must have been barely dawn when the vessel had been captured. She opened her arms wide to embrace the ocean.

There were two large vessels flying British flags on either side of them. One, with the lettering *HMS Brisk*, was tied to the *Violante*. Three-pronged hooks gripped the schooner's railing, and long ropes attached to them led to the cruiser. *The Brisk must be four times as big as we are! And that row of one . . . two . . . three . . . four . . . five guns sticking out of square holes near the cruiser's railing is aimed directly at us! So that was the explosion! Did they hit anything?* She looked around but didn't see any damage. *Perhaps they aimed over the deck, just to scare us? No wonder the Violante didn't put up a fight! What defense would they have against those guns!* She looked up at the *Brisk's* great square sails. *With those guns, and those sails, Kai would call this a sloop-of-war,* she thought.

"What? What monsters! They will crush us!" Sau exclaimed. She had just pulled her head through the hatch, and seen the cruisers for the first time. "Look how close they are, and how high!"

"The sailors must have just leapt onto our deck," said Fima. "No wonder they made so much noise."

There were *Violante* crew members sitting awkwardly on the deck by the cooking shed, or caboose, with their hands manacled behind them. Fima recognized the captain—not so neat now with his cap askew and his uniform soiled—and Señor Barba, without his pipe.

When all the captives were unshackled and on the top deck, they all were given water. The naval officer made another announcement, and again called the Corporal to translate.

To make it less crowded in the hold, the Corporal said, the women and children would remain on deck. The men would stay below, although they would be regularly brought up for air and exercise. The women and girls who were able would help with preparing food. And everyone should be aware that the shackles were still working very well. They would not hesitate to restrain troublemakers at the first sign of any disturbance.

Then all but two of the crew of the *Violante* were transferred to the *HMS Brisk*. Fima and Sau were glad to see Gregorio go. The captain remained shackled on the *Violante*, and the cook would carry on with his work.

Soon Fima heard "Heave ho!" The Royal Navy had taken over the *Violante*, and it was again moving through the water, leaving the two cruisers behind.

CHAPTER 8
A few days later
Travelling toward Sierra Leone

Despite her bony condition, Sau was usually asked to help with cooking. She always came back coughing and with her eyes smarting from the smoke and soot at the large stove—the slave stove, the cook called it. He said all slavers had a slave stove in a caboose on the top deck, and there was no way to work there without becoming covered with soot. After everyone had been served, Fima was helping Sau wipe off when the Corporal sat down near them.

"Why are you the only one wearing a green cap and jacket?" Fima asked him. She pointed to the red and blue coats of the other crew members.

"They are Royal Navy. I am with the Sierra Leone Militia. We are the reserves. The Militia is called whenever the army or navy needs more men, for example, in a situation like this. As soon as the *Brisk* captured the *Violante*, we began referring to her as a "prize." The Navy must provide a separate crew to take over the prize and take it to Freetown so it needs enough extra officers and men to do that. Sometimes they tow it to Freetown instead, but if they do, the cruiser can't go on looking for other slavers."

He smiled. Smiles had a way of slowly growing on his face that Fima couldn't turn away from for fear of missing the next curve of his lips. "Anyway, if we don't find any slavers to capture, I will always be busy playing the bugle calls."

"You play the bugle?" Fima and Sau both opened their eyes wide in surprise.

"Yes. You would have heard me playing calls last night, we were so close, but we wanted our seizure to be under total surprise so we kept quiet. We'd been waiting for you."

"Do you mean you had been waiting for us to come out of the Strait? You didn't just see us by chance in the ocean?"

"Ah, we knew about you long before that. In fact, we came here to find you. The owners of these slave vessels are tricky. They use flags like masks. The *Violante* was in our courts last month with a different name—the *Mary Anne Cassard*—and flying an American flag. That time, she tricked us and the charges didn't stick, so we had to let her go. We've been watching her ever since.

"You saw the other cruiser assisting the *Brisk* this morning? That's the *HMS Bonetta*. Another Portuguese schooner, the *Gertrudes,* loaded up its slaves in the Strait the day before you loaded. The *Bonetta* will stay there until the *Gertrudes* leaves the Strait.

"We stayed with the *Violante* because we are better armed. And we brought the *Bonetta* along to make sure everything went right. The *Violante* is still trying to dupe us—this time she's flying a Portuguese flag. Anyway, this time she won't escape because we caught her red-handed, full of slaves!"

He shook his head. "It seems like there is nothing these slave traders won't try. Maybe someday someone will figure out how to put a mask on a whole slave vessel and make it disappear! That would be the only way they would be able to escape from us!" They all laughed at the idea of such a huge mask.

Fima said, "I'm sure someone has tried it using witchcraft!"

A crew member passed, nodding a greeting and saying, "Corporal."

"'Corporal.' That's a strange name," Sau teased him. "Is that your mask?"

"Mask? For me? Do you think I'm trying to hide something?" Then he laughed. "Oh, I see. So you want to know my name, do you?" He stood up, clicked his heels together, and pretended to tip his cap (*Did he just wink at me?* thought Fima.). "Michael Tosin, at your service."

"Tosin? What kind of name is that?" asked Sau.

"It's really Oluwatosin. It's an Aku name. I was rescued like you. The Navy captured our slaver in the Bight of Benin and brought it to Freetown. I was only twelve then." He laughed, remembering. "That was ten years ago. They had just started the Militia, and were looking for recruits in the Yard. (The Yard is where you stay when you first arrive in Freetown).

"You should have seen me. As soon as they asked, I was the first one to stand up! I was so small and so skinny, but I loved their uniforms! They just laughed at me and said I had to spend some years in school first. So I did, but as soon as they let me, I joined the Militia." Fima smiled to see him remembering. But her neck hurt, and she closed her eyes.

Michael turned to go, saying, "Thank you for cooking the food, Sau. I can tell this rice is from Sherbro—upland rice is considered a delicacy in Freetown. We only find it in the market now and then, and it's expensive.

"Well, there are two more reasons you ought to appreciate it now," teased Sau. "The first is that this rice is from Fima's grandmother's farm. And the second is that Fima donated it—free!"

"Donated it?" Michael asked, looking at Fima. But she had fallen into a restless sleep.

So Sau told him the story of how Fima had been captured. Michael was shocked. "Well, the *Violante* must not be planning to visit Sherbro again. You wouldn't think a vessel would be allowed in the Strait again if it is seizing townspeople! But who knows? They do just about anything.

"Sau, listen to me. You tell Fima that I will take care of what they owe her. When slavers are condemned in Freetown, all the equipment and merchandise is put up for public auction. I'll make sure the court knows the merchandise of this schooner isn't yet paid for. The captain will have to square up before anything can be sold."

CHAPTER 9
Still travelling toward Sierra Leone

In the days before they landed, Sau nursed Fima. She cleaned her wound again and again and tried to persuade her to eat. And to talk.

"You make rope, too, don't you? I can tell by how shiny and smooth your right leg is! It hurts, doesn't it—twisting the fibers on your leg?" Sau pulled up her wrapper to show her own equally shiny left leg. "Just like mine. For me, it's my left leg, because I'm left-handed."

Fima smiled, and reached out to feel Sau's hairless leg. "It pulls all the hair off. Do you make the nets, too? I don't. I send the rope to my grandmother in her village and she makes her own fishing nets and baskets."

"I help my aunt to make them. We fish in a river not far from our village."

Michael was with them one afternoon

when Fima was asking Sau, "You said that the chief only pretended not to know that these women—the founders of the Circle—had been given special authority to do what they were doing. How do you know he knew?"

"Remember the fossils that all disappeared? Well, people say that one still exists. One of the village chiefs has it. They say what happened in that village was that at the time of the founding of the Circle, to get rid of the founder in his village, the chief traded her for a beautiful, engraved box. They say that while she was being taken away he also forced her to hand over her fossil.

"Just the fact that he insisted on taking it, shows that he coveted its power, doesn't it? The story goes that he put the fossil inside the box and buried the box under his rooms. The chiefs in that village have always lived in that same house to guard the spot where the fossil was hidden. As long as the chief is in possession of the fossil, the Circle's authority is in his hands."

"Which village is it? Is it yours?"

"No, not ours. I don't know which one. But everyone in all the villages knows the story. We all know that all the chiefs fear the power of the Circle." Sau laughed. "And in our village at least, that power is about money. I think our chief fears the idea of women who have the power to make money. He does not want that power in our hands."

The *Violante* was at sea for five days before it sailed into the harbour in Freetown in the early hours of New Years Day. The Colony's churchbells were ringing out over the water and happy voices reached them through the morning on the wind. "Tɛl Gɔd tɛnki, mi nɔ day, o!" Praise God! I'm still alive to celebrate another new year! The captives on the ship sang along with them.

But Fima could not sing. The wound under her chin had become so swollen and inflamed that at night it throbbed in her ear and cheek. And even without the handcuff, she could not bear to touch her right hand.

Very soon after they docked, two government officials came aboard. One was the marshall from the court, Michael said. The one in the white coat was a medical officer and he was arranging for those who needed hospital care to leave now for the trek to Kissy, four miles away. When he asked if there were any who would not be able to walk, Michael moved nearer to him and they spoke in low voices, looking repeatedly at Fima.

A porter appeared and dropped a grass hammock on the ground next to her so suddenly that she started. He looked at her, waiting and pointing. Although she had never done it before, she understood that she was to lie on it so she could be carried to the hospital. Then the other porter arrived. They greeted each other—obviously, they were used to meeting up on jobs at the harbour. "Dɛ way! Wla wa mu!"

In her dreamy state of mind, Fima greeted them back as she arranged herself onto the hammock, imagining she was back in her warehouse greeting the Kru porters who came looking for work every day, and not that she was talking to strangers. The two men laughed as they passed the bamboo pole through the hammock, and hoisted it first up to their shoulders and then onto their heads for the journey.

She didn't even hear when one of them said, "This is our own wife, my friend. She speaks our language! Take care with her!"

They set off at full speed down the gangplank and Fima gripped the edge of the hammock with her left hand in terror to try to steady herself. She was swinging from side to side out over the water! But the men did not slow their pace, which soon lulled her to sleep.

Fima knew nothing about the trip from the deck of the *Violante* through Freetown and along the narrow path to Kissy village, up the south side of the hill to the hospital, and into her cot in the ward. She was not aware of how many starts and stops the trip took or of the patients hobbling alongside. She did not see those that fell to the road unable to go further or see the overseer calling more porters to carry them the rest of the way on their backs.

CHAPTER 10
2nd January 1839
Queen's Yard, Colony of Sierra Leone

"Jina!" Sau shouted. "Jina!"

She was waving her arms and trying to break free from the other captives from the *Violante* who were climbing, or being helped, up the seaside rocky entrance into the Queen's Yard. From the moment she entered and raised her head, of all the people seated and lying in the yard, she saw only her sister. They both scrambled to their feet at the two ends of the Yard and spread their arms, and started running; two identical tall Sau's.

"Jina, are you all right? How long have you been here?" Sau asked. Other people in the yard either lay sickly, watching, or started gathering around them, smiling. Perhaps they were happy to see that it was still possible to find relatives in this strange place.

"Look how alike they are!"

"I'm sure even their own mother can't tell them apart!"

"No, the older one—the Sau—the dry, thin one—has a gap in her front teeth. Do you see?"

"What pain for the family, to lose them both!"

"We just arrived," Jina said but she was looking at Sau. She put both hands on her shoulders and brought them gently down her bony arms to hold her hands. "Why are you only just coming now? Where have you been all this time? You left so long ago!"

The registrar had risen from his table and was calling Sau back to wait for her turn to be entered in the register. She didn't even hear him.

Sau said, "I didn't want it to happen to you. What went on in the village after I left?"

"Everything changed for me after you left. I could tell that it was just a matter of time before I was traded, too. The chief started watching me. He just did not trust me anymore, and no one else wanted to associate with me. Can you imagine that even Mariama wouldn't talk to me anymore? So when I slipped at the stream and sprained my wrist one day, and I could only work with one hand, and he said I was being uncooperative, I knew it was going to happen."

"How strange that we met here!" said Sau. "What if our vessels had not been captured?"

"I thought I would never see you again!"

They looked at each other full of wondering. Then Sau straightened up, saying "It's our destiny to always be together. We would have found each other somehow. How is Mother? Father? Our brothers?"

A clerk had come over from the gate. He stood in front of Jina. "Whichever one of you is from the *Violante*, you must return to the queue so you can be registered. Then you will be able to join your sister." They looked at him then, and he smiled at their sameness.

"Your vessels are like twins, too. The *Gertrudes* docked just before the *Violante,* and side-by-side. Both schooners, both flying Portuguese flags. We only just finished registering whoever came on the *Gertrudes*; was that you?" He pointed to Jina. Jina nodded. The girls touched their palms together, and Sau walked back to the gate.

With two full shiploads from the Sherbro River, there was a lot of busy activity in the yard. They cleaned the yard, cooked and served food, and helped with the children. Royal African Corps recruiters came and spoke to all the men, encouraging the ablest ones to join the Corps. And late in the afternoon when the bell rang and the drums beat and the noisemakers sounded in town, food was served, but Jina complained she was being overfed and pushed most of hers toward Sau to finish.

One morning those who were well were asked to line up at the street exit from the yard. Everyone from the *Gertrudes* and the *Violante* would begin doing public works during the day. They would receive 2d in rations every day. As Sau looked around, about half of the people in the yard remained lying or sitting along the walls. Jina's wrist was still swollen, so she was not going. Many were exhausted from long walks or months of not eating well. They gave their names at the gate and moved out for the first time into the city of Freetown.

Everything was new to them. Children and adults passing in the street stopped to watch them climb toward the Cotton Tree. Sau started cutting grass, pulling up weeds and cleaning around this mammoth buttress-root tree, which formed a roundabout where five streets met in the centre of town. From there, they moved on up the hill, where the streets became smaller and more wooded.

In the afternoon when the sun was no longer overhead and a light breeze started cooling resting places between the trees and along the road descending toward the harbour, the bell sounded and they returned to the yard.

CHAPTER 11
15th January 1839
Yagoi

Weeks had gone by. Toby had taken to sleeping in Mama Boi's kitchen whenever he had spent the day working on the Jong River, taking advantage of the fact that the warehouse and house were unoccupied. Imagining that someone had asked him to check the building and clean the compound regularly, and having Laneh bark and jump about so excitedly when they approached the compound, made him feel more hopeful about Fima. The neighbours became used to seeing him there and would come by to say hello and report if they had noticed anything, and share news.

One evening when Toby was leaning down by the fire to give the remainder of his food to Laneh, he heard a noise behind him. He turned to see Fima's mother arriving with porters carrying rice. After their greetings she asked, "Toby, isn't it late for you to be here? Aren't you going home? And. . . " she looked about at the stacked, empty pots in the kitchen, and at the locked door. "Where is Fima?" When Toby didn't answer, she repeated, "Toby, where is Fima?"

And so Toby told her. While the porters stacked the rice in the warehouse, he sat with Mama Boi in the growing darkness explaining how he had searched and searched for Fima. As he talked, she clamped her hands against the sides of her head and cried out, shaking her head from side to side.

"Oh, my child! Thank God her father does not know! Every time I go to the village, he asks me again and again if I am sure Fima is safe, . . . if I should not bring her back near him where there is protection. I always assure him that he has nothing to worry about. I tell him that the slave traders depend on merchants like us. How else would they get rice and beans and farina? And I tell him that Fima is very careful. She doesn't take risks. But he never quite believes me."

"Well, he's her father. We fathers worry about our daughters."

Both of them were quiet, staring into the dark. But it wasn't the dark they were looking at. They were seeing in their minds that determined set to Fima's jaw when she had decided to do something she wanted to do, and the way she tossed her head and stood up straight when she had made up her mind to take action. Could she have had a plan of her own?

The next day they began looking for Fima again. They asked all the neighbours. No one had any new information about her. Banna, and his porters also, claimed to know nothing.

Toby had told Mama Boi about the scrap of material he had found on Laneh, and about the condition the dog was in. She agreed that the cuts and bruises on his body could only mean someone had abused him.

"If Laneh attacked Kai, he would only do it for a reason," Mama Boi said. "Or if the opposite happened—if Kai attacked Fima's dog—that would only happen for a reason, too. What could he have been trying to do?"

"Mama Boi, the only thing I know," Toby said. "is that Kai used to be regular on the waterway, and now they say he is never there. That means he is spending his time on something more profitable."

"He is a boatman, after all. That is the only work he knows. He has to be somewhere on the water."

They travelled by canoe to the busy trading areas in the Strait, asking the boatmen they found for Kai in York Island, Bonthe and Bendu.

One day tired from spending the morning asking questions in Bendu, the two of them walked along the shore. Laneh began sniffing down where the long brown arms of the mangrove arched like the legs of marchers through the water along the shore. He started digging at something in the mud and then began whimpering at it. He ran to Mama Boi, barked at her and then ran back to the spot. Finally he loosened the object and brought it back to her, laying it at her feet.

She picked it up and gasped. She swayed as if losing her balance. Toby rushed to catch her and helped her sit down on a rock. But the shock had happened. She had recognized it immediately, even water-soaked: it was pieces of the old leather and straps from the bundle she had carried for so long.

Fima would never be careless enough to let it drop into the water. She must have drowned. That must also be why Kai was missing; either he was responsible or he, too, had drowned.

Ay, Fima! Fima, Fima! My only daughter! Why did I ever give her the bundle? she asked herself. *I cast my fate on her. The spirit has escaped, and it consumed her. If only I had kept it, whatever was going to happen would have happened to me.*

But in her heart she was saying, *So this was our destiny—to lose Fima!* She was convinced that there was no way fate can be avoided or reversed.

The next day, Fima's mother sent off the shipment of rice and closed the shop. As she snapped the padlock shut, she remembered how Fima's slim, strong fingers looked as she had clamped it shut for her so many times. She thought how Fima had always said she wanted to have her own shop one day with wheeled carts.

There was nothing else to do. She had to go back to the village and explain what had happened. Perhaps the family would arrange for someone else to help her run the shop.

With a slow, heavy tread Mama Boi set off down the road. She could feel her neighbour watching and knew she was too sorry to come out and say goodbye.

CHAPTER 12
A few days later
Kissy, Colony of Sierra Leone

Fima was at the hospital for weeks. She only began coming back in snatches, moving in and out of dreams. She finally began to realise who and where she was.

One night she dreamed that her mother was standing in the road at home, calling for her, "Fima, where is the bundle? What did you do with your Great Grandma Fima's leather packet? Is it still wrapped up tight?"

Fima sat up in bed, panicked. The whole experience came back to her. She had released the evil! Because of her, the family no longer had protection. They were lost and there was nothing anyone could do. Fima curled up on her side, covered her face with her hands, and began to cry. Over and over again she chanted, "'God is our refuge and strength, a very present help in trouble.'" until she fell asleep.

The next morning her first thought was the crack in the knot in the hull. Not what it looked like, but what it felt like in almost total darkness and in fear. Just thinking about the place made her gasp. Then she determinedly forced her mind back. She must understand this. Could she find the small metal piece again? She didn't even really know what it was. She hadn't had a chance to examine it.

And besides, wasn't it a thing? It was not a spirit. Fima had never expected that. Can you touch a family's curse? Put it in your mouth? Does tragedy look like a gold-coloured object?

Nonetheless, it was her mother's, and her grandmother's. She closed her fist in determination. She would get that piece back so she could take it back to her mother.

Someone had entered the ward. He was walking toward her cot. It was Michael! He laughed when he saw her awake and she became calmer when she heard him laugh. He put his cap under his left arm and gave her a mock salute. "New Person, welcome back!"

Fima frowned at him quizzically. "Good morning, Michael."

"You look wary today," he said. "Like

you don't trust me. I think I like you better sleepy," he said slyly. *How did he know what she looked like when she was sleepy?* she thought. But she could tell he was teasing.

"Seriously, Fima, I'm happy to see you looking better. And there's another reason, a very good reason, that I called you 'New Person.' While you were sick, you missed a big event: on the 10th of January the courts condemned the *Violante*, so everyone was freed from slavery. Here they call the freed captives, New People. Or sometimes, the Queen's People."

Fima looked at him without speaking. He looked a little disappointed. His good news didn't have the impact he had expected.

She asked impatiently, "And where is the *Violante* now? And Sau?"

"Ah . . . Sau is well. The Liberated African Department has been taking care of them all in the Queen's Yard since they arrived. And in fact, it is the Department taking care of you here, as well."

"Yes, but how . . . "

"You know, Fima, Sau told me how you were captured. It was terrible. It was a shocking thing. But. . . many of us—" (he was hesitating, but Fima could tell that

Michael wanted very much for her to listen, so she tried to do so.) "many of us—the Liberated Africans—walked hundreds of miles from where we were captured, in chains, before spending many months in the barracoon and then being packed in slavers. In my case, even the prize journey after our capture, the trip to reach Freetown, took eight weeks. And there was fever on board our vessel. Many of us died on the way, including a good friend of mine. I was sure that I would be next.

"It was such a relief when we were released here. In the yard, you have good food. The clothes they give you aren't beautiful, but the food is good and plentiful. There is a fountain there that they call King Jimmy Water. It has better water than you have ever seen at home in Sherbro. Now that your vessel has been condemned, all the *Violante* New People will begin going out to work every day on public works projects like clearing grass and rubbish off the streets, and then when the bell rings in the afternoon, they return.. . .

"Fima, you're upset. What is the matter?"

"But the vessel? What about the *Violante*? Where is it? What happens to the vessels themselves when they are condemned?" Fima asked.

"Do you mean the crew? The Mixed Courts here do not have authority to prosecute crews. By treaty, each country prosecutes its own crews when vessels are conde. . . ."

"No, not the crew!" Fima interruped. "The vessel!"

"The vessel?" Michael couldn't believe her question. "Why? Why do you care?"

Fima looked down at her lap. She could not possibly explain about the scattered bundle and what shame she had brought on her family. She could hear her grandmother saying, "Some things are not meant to be said."

"I beg for your understanding, Michael."

Michael sighed. "Well, they started a new system a few years ago. They take the vessels to a bay where they are scuttled; broken up into pieces . . . " Michael paused because Fima had sat up suddenly, shocked, as if she had seen a ghost. ". . .Uh . . . for good reason, of course. So no one can use them for slave trading again. . . ." He paused again. "Fima, what's the matter?"

But she was staring as if in a trance. Almost inaudibly, she said, "Go on."

"The place where they do this they have

been calling Destruction Bay," he continued. "They saw each vessel up in three pieces and then they auction off the pieces. You can get cheap wood that way to . . . build a house or a . . . river boat."

Michael's voice petered out to silence. Fima had her hands over her mouth and her eyes were wide in horror. "And what about the *Violante*? Have they sawn up the *Violante*?"

"No, I don't think so. Your lien slowed down the public auction of the merchandise. Did Sau tell you about that? The captain has to pay for your rice."

"Yes, she told me. Michael, there is something I have to do. I cannot go and stay in the yard. I cannot stay confined anywhere for two or three months. Please. You have to help me."

"But you're not strong enough to be on your own. Tell me the problem. Let me handle it."

"I can't tell you right now. I just . . . I must go somewhere to hide before they send me to the yard. Where is this Destruction Bay? Is it far from here?"

"It is between here and the harbour where we landed. But there is no place to hide in the bay. It's dangerous to be on the waterfront at night."

"Where else can I go? Where do you live?"

"In fact, I live right near the bay, in Magazine Cut."

"So you can take me home with you."

Michael leant back in his chair and laughed out loud.

CHAPTER 13
Kissy

At the sudden noise, the other patients and their visitors all turned around to look.

Michael drew near and lowered his voice. "Pardon me? Take you home with me? Did I tell you I am the leader of the Militia band? Imagine if I brought a strange woman home! I would lose my position! They're very strict here. And people would say bad things about you," Michael said.

"Strange woman?" Fima laughed. "Me? I'm just a child! I have only just turned sixteen!"

"Child, eh?" Michael replied. "You're not a child. That is a child in the next bed."

But when he and Fima looked, they saw that the bed was occupied not by a child but by an elderly woman. Michael looked around him, confused, and seeing that other patients were listening, he asked, "What happened to that young girl who was in this bed?"

"Hmmph," said a woman across the aisle. "What happened to her, indeed."

Other patients in the ward were agreeing with her. "It's what happens to many of the children who come here."

Just then a nurse entered the ward, and everyone kept quiet until she had left. Then the woman continued in a hoarse whisper, "Last night, the accountant came here in the middle of the night. He brought a woman. He took some money from her and then she took the child away. No paperwork at all."

"People get apprentices for half the fee here that they would pay in the Yard. And they don't sign an indenture contract so they have no obligations," another woman added. "They don't promise to teach them any skills, and they don't even have to send them to school. No one monitors what they do to them!"

"Have you asked what happened to any of the children you have seen leave here? What do they say?"

"They say they were discharged, of course. Returned to their villages. Sent back to the Yard. What can you say to that?"

They all fell silent. Their angry eyes slowly returned to where the conversation began, with the elderly woman lying in the bed. "It wasn't me!" she protested. Embarrassed, they all turned away.

Michael turned back to Fima. "There are many things you need to learn about Freetown. You have not seen the Liberated African Department register book where they entered your name as one of the Queen's People. Any girl over fourteen is listed as a woman. And any boy over fourteen is a man. You are now legally registered as a woman."

Fima stared at him, astonished. Then she sat up straight in her cot and posed, sassily, with her left fist on her hip. "All right, then. If I am a woman, I can get married."

"I was just going to suggest the same thing."

"What same thing?" She studied his face and saw he was serious. "To marry you? You aren't serious, are you? I meant, I could fake getting married. You and I could pretend. If you would do that, I would pay you back for the favor someday. Would you do that for me?"

"No, Fima, I wouldn't. Be quiet and let me explain."

She was annoyed, but he only sat there, waiting, saying nothing, waiting for her to meet his eyes. Finally, she folded her hands and looked at him.

He said, "You need to know more about what will happen to you here," he said. Fima shifted impatiently, and he said, "Are you interested?"

She nodded.

"The Colony is a different kind of place. The three months in the yard is like training. After the yard, the New People are assigned to villages. They try to settle you in a village you will like, where people speak your own language. They will give you some basic supplies, and expect you to construct a house on the small property they give you. But after three more months in the village, they cut off your ration so if by then if you do not have a farm, or a business, or a job, or you are not married, you will not be able to survive.

"Of course, your friends in the village will help you, but they are trying to succeed, too. Most jobs pay 4d to 6d per day. But you have to be careful to stay near people that you know. It is safe in the Colony, but if you leave or are in a remote place by yourself, there is always the risk that someone will capture you and sell you to a slave trader."

"What do you do?"

"As for me, I'm a businessman. I go up country for rice—red rice, swamp rice—to sell in town."

"You do?" she exclaimed, "We send rice to sell in Freetown . . . ." Her voice drifted off into silence as she remembered that she no longer had a shop.

"My friends and I have a cooperative," Michael went on. "We put our funds together so we can buy the whole contents of a condemned slaver at once. The merchandise is cheaper that way. Then we sell it retail either here in town or upcountry. Not everything on the vessel brings money. Salt, for example. There is always a lot of salt because they use it for ballast, so in the end you just give it away. Farina is almost as bad. But there are many other things of value that we can sell."

Michael took her hand, and began to speak more gently.

"And that is not my only income, Fima. As corporal in the band I make 1s 3d per day, and when I am called on duty for training or service, like on the *Brisk*, they increase it to 1s 6d a day."

"Michael, stop! You sound as if you are presenting yourself to my family. I don't want to get married. How can I? None of my family is here." Her breath caught suddenly at that idea. Would she ever see any of them again?

"I am trying to explain that getting married will help you succeed here. Also, if you marry now, you need not stay in the yard.

"And another reason is, uh, I like you, Fima. I like to be with you and you are sensible and independent. You behave like an Aku woman. Like the women I know. They speak up and they are not afraid to try new things.

"I don't want anyone to come in the middle of the night and take you as an illegal apprentice, and I certainly don't want anyone to kidnap you and sell you back into slavery!"

Fima looked at him, and studied his face. In fact, Michael was a nice person. She suspected that he had been coming regularly to see her in the hospital. And she always listened to him when he talked—unlike Kai! Thinking about Kai made her feel a bit guilty. She had forgotten to think about him!

"Michael, what about you? Are your people here? How does anyone get married with no family near? There is no one to ask permission from. No one to attend the ceremony! No one to celebrate!"

"What happens here is that the Liberated African Department will request a marriage license from the surrogate. If the surrogate approves, you go and collect it. Then you go to the church for the ceremony. But if we like, we can just hold the license until we are ready for the marriage ceremony. Would that make you happy? Oh, and I forgot—for the license, you need an English name."

"What? Why? Where can I get an English name?"

"It's not difficult. How about . . . Rebecca? Rebecca Thomas. How is that for a name? She was a teacher I had when I first arrived here."

"But I like my name. Fima was my great-grandmother's name. She was the wife of a chief. I want to keep it."

"Your English name is just for doing English things, like signing the marriage license. I will never call you anything but Fima," he said, squeezing her left hand because the other was still bandaged. "Fima, I must go now. I have to be on the Parade Ground on Water Street in time for the bell. The band practises every day just after the workday is finished."

In three days, on the 21st of January,

when Michael collected the license from the surrogate court, the clerk said, "But you're not dressed up. And where is Rebecca? Aren't you getting married today? Most people go straight on to the church."

"Rebecca's in the hospital right now," Michael replied. "We are going to postpone the ceremony for a bit."

CHAPTER 14
23rd January 1839
Central Freetown

In the middle of the afternoon five days later, Fima was just approaching King Jimmy market on Water Street in central Freetown.

She wanted to cook that day for Michael. He had been trying so hard to help her! He had had clothes sewn for her so that she could walk decently out of the hospital yesterday, and he had provided a room for her next to his half-constructed stone and frame house in Magazine Cut. He was willing to postpone their wedding until she was ready for it.

Thanks to Michael's insistence, the court had ordered another search of the captain's cabin of the *Violante*, and under a cupboard there they had found Banna's note. So there was no doubt what was owed to Fima, and her mother's rice money would be paid soon.

Atlantic Ocean

Destruction Bay

Magazine Cut

Harbour
Water St
Queen's Yard
Tower Hill

Kissy

And—best of all—she was walking free in the street again, all because of Michael!

But Fima had another reason for her outing this morning. She had specifically asked about Water Street. *If you get lost, just ask for the Parade Ground,* Michael had said. So if anyone asked, she wouldn't have trouble explaining wanting to see Water Street for herself. It was the most popular street in town, running parallel to the ocean, twice as wide as the others and lined with merchant shops.

Down Water Street, at the opposite end from the Parade Ground, was the entrance to the Liberated African yard, and that yard was the real reason Fima had set her sights on Water Street today. She wanted to talk to Sau.

Fima had spent some time at the Parade Ground and she agreed with Michael. *It's a beautiful, wide, grassy place with cannon facing out to sea along one side. The Militia has inspections there, and you'll see lots of other activity.* It seemed to be the crossroads for any man, woman, child or animal that had anywhere to go in Freetown.

But now she had moved down the street as far as the bridge that overlooked all the waterside activity of King Jimmy market. It made her feel good to hear the clamour of familiar everyday life. Traders and customers passed up and down the steps that had been dug into the hillside that led up to where she stood.

But Fima turned. She moved on past the market to Queen's Yard at the end of the street. At the entrance, she called out a greeting. A rectangular flap opened at eye level in the post house. The sentinel yawned and rubbed his eyes. The New People were not there. He couldn't say exactly where the New People were working today. He did not know where they would be working tomorrow. After the flap closed again and he didn't open to check if she had gone, Fima moved carefully forward to peer inside the yard.

She was surprised at how clean it looked. There were New People there sitting and lying about. They did not look very well. Perhaps they were too sickly to work, she thought. Along the far right wall, a blacksmith was working, and she imagined he was the one who would have provided tools for them to work on the roads. She wondered where Sau usually sat, and who she talked to. Looking up, she met the eyes of two white officers looking down into the yard from the next building, which she had decided when she had passed it, was a gaol. She hid her face and ducked backwards into the street.

She had arrived early. They must be still out working. Michael had said they would not return to the Yard until the bell rang at 4:00. She would wait, and in the meantime, she could go to the market.

This time she headed down the irregular dirt steps. She talked to the traders on her way to the fish market at the waterside, asking where their wares came from: leafy vegetables, okra, eggplant, onions, hot peppers, palm oil, groundnut oil, baskets of dried fish, quarts of oysters, heaps of cockles, live chickens, eggs, balls of fufu, heaps of yams, sweet potatoes, coco roots, and plantain. And *agidi* wrapped in banana leaves, and ginger cakes, and tallow candles and palm-nut oil for lamps. And there was upcountry rice, and Sherbro rice. You could buy it by the king's cup, the pound, or by the heaped-up bushel. Fima bit a few grains and broke one with her nails, to see how fresh it was.

When she entered the covered fish market, Fima paused until her eyes had adjusted to the light. On one side were beef traders dressed in caps and long gowns she already knew from Magazine Cut and Fourah Bay. She went over to the fish tables and explained what she needed. They agreed on a price. As the trader brought a heavy piece of wood down onto the back of her knife to cut off the chunk of barracuda for Fima, the voice of the customer standing beside her made her spin around.

It was Sau, leaning around her to ask the trader for a chunk of the same fish but showing no sign that she recognized Fima! Then, suddenly bumped by the person next to her, Sau fell sharply sideways into Fima, and Fima fell onto the person on her other side. Holding onto the rough board of the fish table, Fima was able to hold still until Sau could stand up. Sau said, "I beg your pardon, *ya*? It's very crowded in here." Fima was bewildered. Why didn't Sau recognize her? Had Sau died and become a ghost? Or was Fima a ghost?

But the middle-aged woman on Fima's other side was on the ground, and had not moved. She sat there indignant, making no effort to get up, inspecting her bruised elbow and rearranging her headtie. Her parcels had scattered and she had collided with other women approaching the table. When Fima reached out to her, and helped her to stand and collect her belongings the woman surprised her by shouting to the crowd, "Who pushed us?"

She looked past Fima. Fima turned to see what she was looking at. Among all the women in their traditional dress, her eyes fell on Sau who, without jewelry and in her stiff government-issue canvas looked like an egg left unhatched in a brood of chicks. The woman flipped her hand palm up, gesturing accusingly at Sau while she continued to speak to the women around her. "Do you all see this? Mammy Marie, Aunty Ajara, do you see? Isn't this what we've been talking about? This is what happens when you fill the town with all these unbrought-up Africans from who-knows-where."

Fima moved away from the woman, and slipped partially behind Sau. Under cover of their clothes, she lightly took hold of Sau's left hand. Sau turned to see who she was.

"You're so right!" shouted out another woman. "Hundreds of illiterates descending upon us every day! First they create the colony for us, then they overwhelm us with these people, and give them advantages they never thought of giving us. And before you know it they are taking over everything."

The trader had wrapped Sau's fish and was handing it to her when the woman who had fallen said in an accusing voice, "So! Even the best fish is for them!"

Several women pushed forward to see and made sounds of agreement. "Just look at the size of that chunk! And such fresh barracuda!"

"That is why more and more now, by the time you reach the table, they tell you there is no more fish for today!"

The crowd was growing larger. Everyone looked angry. The girl selling the fish turned to meet the eyes of an older woman sitting behind her, who shook her head slightly. The girl turned back. Without looking up she drew the package back before Sau could take it, and handed back her money. Fima pulled sharply on Sau's left hand, then dropped it and started moving toward the door. She glanced back to be sure Sau was following her.

"Just look at her," they heard someone say as they left. "They come here looking like this but before you know it they are sending their children to England to study!" said one, angrily.

When they reached outside, the girl turned to her. "Th-thank you," she said.

"Who are you?" They were both trembling.

"Who am I?" Fima asked. "Who are you? Aren't you Sau?"

But even mentioning her name, Fima clapped her hands together in recognition. "Of course I know who you are! You're her twin! You're Jina, aren't you? No wonder you didn't know me! How did you get here?"

But Jina could not even answer, she was trying so hard to stop crying. "I-I h-have to buy fish for the Yard. There will b-be nothing to cook. But how c-can I go back in there?"

Fima gave Jina her own fish, assuring her she would buy more for herself on her way home. As quickly as they could they made their way up the rough steps to the street, and there they stopped at a bench under a mango tree.

A cool breeze blew off the ocean. Jina was still trying to get control of herself and Fima bought them both half-ripe coconuts. She watched Jina drink hers in the changing rays of the sun made by the waving leaves. They handed the coconuts back so the trader could split them open and carve out the jelly for them.

"They hate us so!" Jina finally said. "And it wasn't even my fault! Someone pushed me!"

"I know," Fima said. "But they don't really hate us. If that one woman hadn't been there, there would have been no problem. Actually, they need us. I have been learning about how the markets here get their goods. Fish and fufu come to this market from across the estuary twice a week." She pointed out to sea where they could see a strip of hazy blue land in the distance. "And almost all the other produce that you saw down there either is grown in Liberated African villages, or the Liberated Africans bring it from up county. Here in town there is little room to plant anything but cassava. Really, they need us."

They began to talk about other things. The twins had spent a fortnight in the Yard now. And even though some of the men had been recruited for the Royal African Corps—Fima had seen the RAC on guard at the hospital in Kissy—and some of the children had been chosen as apprentices and issued indentures by the Department, the number of people in the yard had not decreased. It was getting more and more crowded. It was hard now even to find a place to sit. During the past week the *Magdalene* and the *Ontario* had also been condemned, each one adding hundreds more Liberated Africans to the Yard.

"What do you all do?"

She shrugged. "Many are quite sick. We have even offered a few of them food only to find out they had died there, where they first sat when they came off their slaver. But many are out most of the day on public works. And the overseers keep telling us they did their annual whitewashing just a few months ago so we should keep the Yard clean."

She thought for a minute. "Of course, we cook. And people just find things to do. Some make things they can sell. Some cut cloth from their *lappas* to make small things like *kotokus*."

"They give you needles and thread?"

Jina showed her the frayed edge of her *lappa*. "You can just pull the thread from the cloth. Some work with the blacksmith. Some carve handles for hoes or knives or cutlasses.

"Sau and I make fishing net rope; one of the cooks brings us *gbameh* tree stalks. There is plenty of water to soak them to get the fibre."

As she explained to Jina where she was living and why she had not returned to the Yard, Fima kept finding herself smiling. It was hard to see her like a stranger, because Jina seemed so familiar to her.

Soon, Jina stood. She was smiling now, and gave Fima a hug. The food must be finished when everyone returned to the Yard, she said. "Thanks to you, we will have fish in our food! Thank you for saving me! I was just too frightened to move!"

They arranged that Fima would meet them both working on Tower Hill tomorrow. "Please tell Sau that I need her help," Fima repeated. "I have something important to ask her. And do you have rope you have finished making? Bring it tomorrow. Maybe I can sell it for you."

After she had gone, Fima stayed under the tree. The brightness of the afternoon had dimmed—surely it was about time for the bell. Suddenly, there was a loud clanging from the Yard and from everywhere else around her, too. That must be the 4 o'clock bell, she thought. She had hoped they would be passing by her on Water Street, but instead they came down the street near the gate. They suddenly appeared with their tools on their heads and in the same roughly-sewn duck canvas clothing as Jina had been wearing, at the end of Water Street, gave their names and disappeared inside.

Fima approached as far as a tree near the gaol adjacent to the yard. Looking down at her own bright *lappa*, she felt a bit ashamed for looking so fine, but then reminded herself that she was no different. Like them, she had no clothes of her own apart from what had just been given to her.

From her shelter, half hidden by the tree, she watched. Some looked bewildered. A few talked and joked. When she saw Sau, Fima gripped the tree to keep from jumping out and shouting her name. Sau looked stronger now.

As they entered the Yard gate, they called out their names for the gateman to mark their arrival. Fima could hear the sentinel shouting a response, but she did not have to be standing nearby to know that he did not even raise his groggy eyelids to look out of the small window of his gate house.

CHAPTER 15
24th January 1839
Magazine Cut

Michael came out of his door the next morning in full uniform. He was carrying a duffel bag and some tools. Fima was startled. Was he leaving? She had come to enjoy seeing him every morning, and had been proud he liked the shine-nose stew she'd cooked for him the day before.

At the bottom of the steps he turned to put the saw, hammer and other things away in the shed. He crossed the compound and entered Fima's room. He dipped into her *kɔntri pɔt* clay cooler in the corner, took a drink of the cool water, and sat down.

"I heard you working on your house last night," she said.

"Yes, now that the ground floor has reached ten feet, I am eager to change from the stone and build the frame structure. It will have verandas front and back. I know you will like it!"

Fima was looking at his bag. He was quiet a minute, then he said,

"Fima, orders just came for me. I should report on another cruiser today, so you will not see me for a while. I'm sorry to leave you so soon. I have left the marriage license on the table for you, in case anyone asks you what you are doing in my compound."

"I will miss you, Michael. God go with you. I hope you will not be gone long."

He smiled when he heard these words. "So, today is the day you are going to see Sau. Do you remember how to get there? You remember where I told you Tower Hill was, or Barrack Hill, as they call it? Just keep walking toward the Cotton Tree. You'll see it there, with barracks and other high buildings on top, and a flat, open area with an old tower and the gallows tree on it.

The grass always needs cutting back along the roadside and the slopes, so I'm sure the New People will have plenty to do today. And you won't miss them! Even though the town is so populated these days, hundreds of people all dressed alike and all doing the same thing would be hard to miss!"

He paused a minute. "I passed by the bay last night when I was coming home," he said.

"The *Violante* was there." Fima's eyes widened and she looked sharply at him. "That means she'll be broken up on Saturday."

It's Thursday today, Fima thought. *I have two days.*

"I'm only telling you because it seems to matter to you," Michael said. "I wish you'd tell me why."

Fima dropped her eyes to the ground, and said nothing. How could she say *I brought evil to my family? There is a curse on me.* He would think that she had fetish beliefs.

"Fima, just promise me that you won't go to the bay by yourself. I'll be back soon. The Royal African Corps are not very good at maintaining security in the Magazine area, and especially not in the bay. The sentinels and constables don't always stay at their assigned posts, especially after dark. In fact, some of them even work for the slave traders. And there are lots of creeping plants that hang over the edge of the cliff that drops to the sand—or to the ocean, when the tide is in. It's hard to see the edge and it would be very easy to fall. It's just a good place to avoid."

Fima promised.

After he had left, Fima prepared herself

to go to town. But when she left the house, her market bag in hand, she turned not west along Fourah bay Road toward town, but down past Guard Street toward the waterside, toward Destruction Bay.

She wouldn't enter the bay, she told herself. She just wanted to see. She had to see the *Violante* for herself.

She climbed up onto some boulders overhanging the beach. She was hidden by a clump of evergreen trees that pricked her face when she parted their thin branches and silky needles.

And it was true! Two schooners were beached now that the tide was out. The *Violante* was on the far side. The other one was already half broken-up. Scattered all over the beach were pieces of timber and odds and ends. Children were rummaging for scraps, and splashing each other in the water. Two RAC soldiers stood near them. Far to the left, two vultures had found a small animal to devour.

Suddenly, two men's voices rose from below her. One particular gravelly voice made her hands fly to her head. Her legs collapsed as she recognized him and the flimsy branch she for support was no good at all. It was Gregorio! She leant closer to hear.

"You're right, Robles," said a British voice. "The *Violante* shouldn't be here. It should be waiting for purchase at the government wharf. We only have a break-up treaty with the Spanish so if a slaver was flying any other flag, we can't break it up."

He paused. "Actually, I do know how the confusion came in. The *Violante* was really a Spanish schooner. It was coming from a Spanish port and returning to a Spanish port and it had a Spanish crew. But it had the papers and the flag to pretend it was Portuguese. So we can't break it up.

I will ask the marshall of the court about this. He is supposed to come along with any vessel brought here. He shouldn't have made such a mistake."

Fima couldn't see Gregorio. She tried to move closer, so she could hear better but suddenly, her foot slipped! Small stones rolled down along the side of her cliff. She held her breath for a minute, but no one looked her way, and she relaxed.

"So my offer will be accepted?" This was a Spanish voice.

"Play your cards right at the auction, Mr. Robles, and no doubt you will get the *Violante* for less than £200..."

"I must have this vessel! I am late returning to Cuba already. Will it be safe from vandals here overnight?"

"Don't worry, it's safe. This bay is well guarded. No one is allowed near the vessels, and it'll be back in the government wharf early tomorrow morning without fail."

Fima bit her lip. In the morning?! The *Violante* would be gone by early morning! So it was tonight or never!

Suddenly, her head snapped back, wrenched by the hair. She fell onto the boulders. There, holding a dagger to her throat, was Gregorio. He was sneering at her. "Why you here? You think I not hear you?"

"Gregorio! You, man! Where are you? What are you doing up there? Gregorio!" Robles called in a loud whisper.

He sighed disgustedly, and lifted his dagger off her throat. Still holding her hair, he reached inside his torn trousers pocket and pulled out an iron collar, with its swinging iron bar. Then, releasing her, he took out the key. He opened the collar and threatened to come near. Fima had backed up as far as she could. She drew her feet up close to her chest, closed her eyes and tightened herself up into a ball. When she looked up he was climbing down the slope, leaving her trembling like the long needles on the trees.

"Is this the man you told to meet us here?" Mr. Robles whispered again as Gregorio approached.

"Si, it is him," he replied.

Fima turned. She could see them now. The speaker, a tall, casually dressed man, had come out from under her overhang and was pointing to an African who was approaching across the beach. The British man had gone.

Robles spoke to the African. "We're sailing for Havana in a fortnight. According to what I have heard, they do not permit any vessel to leave Freetown with more people on board than will make up a crew. Is that true? Gregorio, here, is telling me different."

"Ah, well," the stranger began, rubbing his chin and leaning on one leg, "as you know, it all depends. Arrangements can be made. If you are willing to pay for them, that is." He smiled, but Robles's face did not change expression. "Just five or six miles out of the harbour, you could easily come across a canoe or two taking slaves from Sherbro to the groundnut and rice plantations on the northern rivers. It depends on whether the canoes make it past the village managers at Kent and Wellington. If they do, you will get at least 100, if not 200 slaves from each canoe, at the best rate there is.

"But you understand, there is risk for them. The Colony seaside village managers are always out cruising for them, and the traders charge for the risk."

"Can I trust the boatmen? How do I know they will not have Royal Navy men on board?"

"They are not in the trade to trap you, my man! They only want your money! I can think of two boys right now who make a good business of slaving up and down the coast: one is called Salieu and the other is Kai. They are sharp, but they are in it for the money."

Kai? Fima's heart began to pound, and she stopped listening. *My Kai? In the slave trading business? But he works on the Bum-Kittam waterway!* A picture flashed into her mind then of Kai in his blue African clothes standing talking to Banna, after she had been captured on the *Violante. Could he have gone back to Banna for payment?*

Fima suddenly felt a cold, hard place in her chest. Dully, she realised the men were still talking.

"And what about provisions? We'll need food to get them to Cuba."

"Just let me know the amounts you need."

The men were moving off down the beach. Gregorio, following them, turned and looked up where he knew Fima was hidden. He took hold of his trousers pocket and clanked the manacles at her. From her hiding place, Fima thought he must be able to hear her bones clanking back.

CHAPTER 16
Tower Hill

"S-s-s-s-s! S-s-s-s-s!"

Four or five New People on Tower Hill turned around to see who was calling. Two were up the slope cutting back underbrush with cutlasses. Fima had been trying to make herself heard over the chopping and the chinking of hoes against the gravel and the sh-shuing of palm brooms on the dry ground.

"Fima!" one of them shouted, in a whisper. She looked up and down the curve in the road before crossing over. Fima had seen a constable moving up and down the road from time to time making sure no one harrassed or captured any of them, but none was around now.

"Ah. . . " Fima held back, unsure. "You're Sau, right?"

Sau smiled. "Yes, Jina is further up the hill. She said to give you this." She pulled a large roll of fishing-net rope out from under her loose clothing. "It would be wonderful if you could sell it."

She gestured at Fima's clothes. "You look so beautiful! We belong to the Ugly Crew. Do you want to join? Dues are just 5s apiece," and she held out her hand, smiling. The two women near her laughed.

Fima laughed too, but said, "Sau, you know there is no difference between us: if I had not been given these clothes I would have nothing to wear either, the same as you."

Sau smiled and said teasingly, "Given by Michael, am I right? Jina told me about your love match! I always knew Michael was only interested in you! Are you married?"

She came closer then, and spoke in a lower voice. "Fima, Jina told me how you helped her in the market yesterday. She is so helpless in a situation like that! She never could sass anyone. She does not know how to defend herself. I don't think she even knows any unkind words. What would have happened if you had not got her out of there? And we have Michael to thank that you were not wearing government-issue clothes too, so you could help her."

"It was scary for both of us, but it's a

good lesson. We need to keep our eyes open wherever we go. Only children have the idea that the whole world loves them." Fima was having trouble stuffing the rope into the shopping bag she had brought to hold it. She was still trembling from her encounter with Gregorio, and kept looking behind her to see if she was being followed.

"What's wrong? Fima, what's the matter with you?"

Sau became alarmed just looking at her, and as she talked, Sau's eyes grew wider and wider. Fima explained who she had just met, but then explained that she had no choice. She had to go back for something important she had hidden inside the *Violante*. She must go, for her mother's sake, but she couldn't go alone. Would Sau come with her? She had to go right inside, into the hull of the slaver.

And it had to be done at night. Tonight.

At that, Sau changed. Before Fima's eyes she was no longer the new, stronger Sau. She changed back into the thin nervous Sau that she had first met in the hull. She was shaking her head and stiffly backed up, her arms out straight, keeping Fima as far away as possible.

"Sau, I need you. I can't go there alone.

You are the only one I can ask. The *Violante* is in the bay near where I live, and they are taking it away in the morning. You must come with me now so we will be ready! Tonight is our only chance. I promised Michael I would not go to the bay alone, although I didn't tell him why I want to go there."

"Please, Sau. Will you help me? I'm begging you."

Sau hesitated. Then she said, "How can I leave? They won't miss me here, but they will notice when I don't come back to the yard. They check us in to be sure that nothing happened to us during the day."

"Tell Jina to answer twice when she enters the gate, first for you and then for herself. I have seen that gateman. He will never notice. And by now, he will be used to the idea that your voices sound the same."

Sau smiled. "Where did you learn that trick? Oh, I know, Jina must have told you! She and I used to play it if only one of us arrived home on time. Mama would always be in the kitchen so she wouldn't see us when we called out to greet her."

"So you already know will work! If it fools your mother, it will fool anybody. Go and tell Jina now. But don't tell her what we're going to do, in case the trick is discovered and they start asking her questions."

Then Fima thought, *Mistake, Fima! Twins probably never keep secrets from each other.* "You can tell Jina about it tomorrow, Sau. But for today, just tell her you're staying overnight with your friend, and that you'll join the team again tomorrow, ok? Tell her not to worry."

Sau went up the hill to talk to Jina, while Fima waited. The last leathery leaves were falling heavily around her from the *wetman banga* tree she was standing under. She stepped on some just to hear the loud crunch she knew they would make. But then in her mind she could see her little black goat in Yagoi noisily chomping them down. She whimpered a half-sob but then stopped herself, surprised. *Fima, don't be a baby! How can you miss a goat?*

There were so many other things to think about. The clanking irons in Gregorio's soiled pocket rang loud in her ears. She stood straight, and tossed her head. What had she just said to Sau? Tell Jina not to worry? She should listen to her own advice. Busily, she opened her shopping bag again and took out the orange and yellow *docket* and *lappa* she had brought for Sau to slip on for the walk to Magazine Cut.

CHAPTER 17
Magazine Cut

Not long after Fima and Sau had set out from the centre of town at Tower Hill, they heard the ringing of the 4 pm bell. They walked out Kissy Street past the Clock Tower and through the grid of streets to Aku Town at Magazine Cut. They walked in starts and stops as they talked and people had to walk around them.

By the time they reached Michael's compound, it was beginning to grow dark and Fima had been able to convince Sau just why she had to recover the gold piece, hopefully still lodged in the crack in the hull, for her mother.

"If I am going to help you, remember, it's only for you," Sau said. "because fate made us share the same shackles. Because fate brought you and Jina to the same fish table yesterday. I would not do this for anyone else."

Fima gave her a hug, and they walked on in silence.

The gate to the compound was in front of them when Sau asked, "How will we even get into the vessel? Do you have a boat to take out to meet her?" But turning around to answer, it was not Sau Fima saw behind her but their round-cheeked neighbour, holding a food basket covered with a soft flowered cloth. Fima smiled, thankful that they had been speaking in Sherbro.

"Mammy Ayo, good evening!" Fima said. She truly was glad to see a friendly face this evening. "Meet my friend, Sau." To Sau, she said, "Mammy Ayo is our wonderful neighbour. She lives in that house next door."

"Welcome, welcome! I'm glad Fima has a friend already," Mammy Ayo said. "I know Michael likes his pepper soup, so today I made enough soup and *agidi* for all of us." Both of their faces brightened at the aroma and the sight of the wrapped corn paste when she lifted the lid.

By the time they had thanked her and their neighbour had turned back for home, Fima had still not mentioned that Michael was away. It did not seem necessary, somehow.

Fima answered Sau's question. "At low

tide, at about 10 o'clock this morning I would not have needed a boat, so twelve hours later should be the same."

"How do you imagine that we are going to climb on board a schooner on sand in these clothes?" Sau asked.

"We are not," Fima said with a twinkle, as she lit the palm-oil lamp in her room. "As my Grandma always says, 'A woman's hamper is never left behind.'" And from under her bed, she pulled out a bundle which she opened to reveal two pairs of Michael's trousers, two men's shirts, and two caps. All dark coloured, to match the night. Sau shook her head and sat down.

Fima and Sau ate and then lay down, exhausted from the long walk. "Just a short nap," Fima said. Giving herself up to sleep, she smiled to think how shocked her mother would be to hear she had eaten a neighbour's food. And how she would frown to find that there was no pestle behind her door!

They knew nothing more until a shout in the street woke them. It was followed by a thud and the yelp of a dog, and the noise of his bolting away. Fima picked up the lamp and motioned for Sau to follow her as she headed outside for the shed.

The thing that had delighted Fima most about Michael's house had been the shed. It was one of the first places Michael showed her when she came. It smelled of the ocean, and of fishing shacks. She laughed at how his eyes sparkled when he showed her what he had been collecting, and where it all came from. "You can especially find things now that they have been breaking up vessels in the bay," he said. "It is getting harder and harder to find people in the Colony who have the skills to fix things. Often you have to figure out how to do mechanical jobs yourself. The more equipment you have to help you, the better."

Once inside, Fima moved things aside until she found just what she had been looking for. First, she took out a grapple hook. One look at Sau told Fima that she, too, was thinking of the hooks the *HMS Brisk* had used to capture the *Violante.* Then Fima took hold of a narrow piece of wood and pulled on it. It was what she was looking for: a rope ladder, like she had used to climb onto the *Violante,* but short. Just as Sau started to protest, Fima rummaged in the pile and found one, two, three, four and five more rungs that she had seen, with holes in each end. And then she reached for the bag she had brought with her. She pulled out the rope that Sau and Jina had made in the Yard.

"Ah, now I see!" said Sau in a mocking tone. "You never intended to sell that rope, did you? You had a plan for it the whole time!"

"We can still sell it, Sau. We just have another use for it, first. Come, let's take it back to my room. We have some work to do."

So Fima and Sau set to work extending the two ends of the rope ladder and attaching rope to the hooks, by the light of the lamp in her room. When they were finished, they began to dress in Michael's clothes. Fima had to roll up the trouser legs, but Sau's fit just fine. With their hair plaited tightly, the caps covered their heads well. Fima's hands fell on her new earrings. She removed them, and put them in her pocket.

Sau picked up a hook. "How do you think they throw these things, anyway?" she asked, twisting her wrist and trying different angles.

"Come, let's go," said Fima. "I know you'll find a way. We will be back before we have a chance to think about it. If you think I'm going to waste any time inside that slaver, . . . I'm so glad you'll be with me to stand guard outside!"

They wrapped the ladder in one *lappa* and the hook in another. She looked at a heap of elephant grass on the veranda. "We can't use a torch, so there is no use taking grass with us to make one," Fima said.

"The moon will help, except while you're inside . . ." Sau's voice dropped off. She went to the corner of the room where Fima's utensils were sticking out of a pot, and picked up a cooking knife. She passed it from one hand to the other, and weighed it in her right hand. "You need some better knives. They make them in the Yard. I'll get one for you." She wrapped the blade in Mammy Ayo's flowered cloth and put it in her pocket. Her eyes rose and met Fima's.

They were both holding their breath. What unknown danger might this night hold?

CHAPTER 18
Destruction Bay

Their bundles on their heads and their hands on the gate, the two girls paused to listen. Mami Ayo was pounding something in a mortar next door. Passersby talking softly together tramped along the gravel path. Then it was quiet.

Sau started out, balancing her head load by moving her head quickly to one side when she stepped on a small stone. Fima suddenly pulled her back and closed the gate again. In the light of the half moon and without making a sound, she demonstrated moving her shoulders more as she walked, and with long strides, man-like. Sau nodded, and copied her and her bundle fell off her head. The cap fell off, too. They both smothered giggles.

Fima helped her fit her hair back inside the cap. Then, with their bundles tucked instead under their arms, they started out again, two young men off in the night.

Fima led the way along the route she had passed that morning until they reached her lookout with the trees. Just as she thought, there wasn't a guard to be seen near the two vessels. The green-and-white *Violante* was on the far side. Pointing to warn Sau of the loose gravel she had disturbed that morning, Fima did not go back to the road but led the way through the bushes above the high tide mark toward the mangrove on the far side of the bay.

Their feet sank into the mud, and they removed their sandals. Once hidden from the moon along the dark side of the vessel, they unwrapped their loads, and Sau took out the grapple hook. She had turned back into the mangrove and climbed a smooth rock when they heard some boys up further on the beach. Fima went back and they both crouched low in the mangrove, scraping themselves on the oysters and barnacles on the trunks.

They waited till all was quiet, and then Sau took the chance. Spinning the hook around twice in a large circle, she released it. It hit the side of the vessel with a loud bang in the quiet night, and fell to the sand. They looked at each other in panic, waiting. No one came. Sau went to get the hook and returned to her position. She threw it again, by flipping her wrist outward. This time it went high enough, but did not reach the vessel, and fell back on the sand. Fima started thinking about what might happen if . . . but she shut her mind to anything except what Sau was doing. Sau threw it again with the same flip of her wrist, and this time, it held. Not one, but two prongs had firmly taken hold of the gunwale. They pulled on the rope ends until the ladder went right to the top. They stared at the ladder: the bottom end dangled above their heads. It was too short.

"Don't worry. I'll give you a hand up," whispered Sau. "How are you feeling? Do you want me to come?"

"No, you stay and watch. I'll be listening for your three taps.

"Wh. . . what was that?" They both stepped back from a thump. It seemed to come from inside the hull. They slogged wildly like big gawky waterbirds through the mud back into the mangrove, and crouched down. Fima's arms were coated in mud now and looked bright in the moonlight.

They watched and waited. Nothing but the water moved. After several waves, a bigger one came in that moved the vessel against a rock with a clunk. "Ah, that was it," Fima said, breathing out. Sau nodded.

They went back under the ladder and Fima waited for Sau to make a cradle with her hands. Instead, Sau put her hand upright, with her palm facing Fima. Fima looked at it, and then put hers up to match it. "We're in this together," said Sau. "I'm for you and you're for me. Here. Take the knife. Maybe you will need it somehow."

"No, you keep it, Sau. You will be alone out here. Remember not to show yourself to anyone!" Then she leapt, using Sau's rising cradle to reach the ladder so she could pull herself up. Once she had a firm grip, she paused and looked up at the top of the ladder, hooked on the railing. She could not believe that she had been so foolish as to climb up the ladder from the longboat. How could she have thought that she would be paid! In the clouds moving in the night sky, she could almost see Gregorio's huge hand reaching out over the railing for her. She tossed her head to wipe out the memory. Looking down at her feet, she made herself climb up to the next rung, and the next. From then on she concentrated on pulling herself up the ladder and up over the gunwale.

On the deck the moonlight was so bright Fima felt like a performer on a stage. She crouched so she would not be so visible, and crawled toward the hatchway. This was where she had fainted! She took hold of the handle and pulled. It didn't move. She pulled on one of the iron crossbars, but instead of opening the hatch the heavy bar came loose. She set the bar down to one side of the hatch and rubbed her right wrist. It was weaker than her left. She crouched over the handle and with both hands she pulled up. The door raised, and she laid it open.

The stench was still there. It rose from inside like a living thing. It pushed her back. She turned away, fighting off the urge to vomit. It had taken her back to that day again, to the stink of Gregorio's sweat, the weight of the iron around her neck, and the moaning of the people in the hold.

Fima, concentrate. This is not sunlight shining down on you. It's moonlight. No one is forcing you to do this. You want to do it. She stepped forward, took hold of the ladder, and put her foot onto the first rung. And the second. Rung by rung, she lowered herself. She was depending only on feel now, and closed her eyes to focus herself. When she felt her feet touch the next deck and she remembered all the manacled feet of the people she had seen here, she bent over and vomited.

Then she told herself again, *Fima, that man is not here! There is no iron around your neck!*

She wiped her face on Michael's long sleeve, and rested her cheek against the familiar material and its comforting smell. All was quiet around her. Fima got onto her hands and knees, closed her eyes, and said in her mind, "This is for my mother. 'God is our refuge and strength, a very present help in trouble.' 'God is our refuge and strength, a very present help in trouble,'" she quoted.

She opened her eyes again, calmer now, but it was just as dark as when they were closed. She heard a scratching noise near the wall of the hull. Then a scampering. And more scratching. Rats! She moved forward slowly, feeling for the second ladder so she would not fall. When she found it, she turned around and began going down.

When had she closed her eyes again? She couldn't remember. Perhaps with them closed, she could feel better with her fingertips. A whiff of a breeze touched her wrist as if something had run past, and she heard more pattering and scraping. She snatched her hands off the ladder as if it were hot. *Rats, you stay away from me!*

When she reached the bottom, she held onto the ladder while she felt with her other hand for the plank. Then she realised how long it was. How would she ever find the place in this dark? She wanted to get out of there!

Fima edged herself down the shelf as far as she felt Gregorio had brought her and then began patting the shelf with her open palms. All the irons were there. Hers and Sau's were smaller than everyone else's, child-size. Michael and the other officer had said so when they were releasing them. That should be easy to find. She climbed up onto the shelf and began moving sideways down the plank like a crab, tapping until she found each one of the cuffs and checking the size.

Then they were there. She had found them, her own cuffs, the child's cuffs that were too small for her.

CHAPTER 19
Destruction Bay

"Ha!"

Rough hands slammed down on one of her ankles. Fima stopped breathing.

"I tell master you no good. You make plan. What you do?"

That smell! It wasn't just the people she had smelled, it was him! His sweat, his dirty clothes, his sour food. She had known he was there!

But now there was a different smell too. She knew that smell. Gregorio had been drinking, and this time Fima was not handcuffed. At least, not yet.

She couldn't let him near the handcuffs. She flipped around, slamming her left heel against the side of his face. He went over sideways. He must have hit the plank, because there was a sharp noise and then she heard nothing.

She turned over and crawled forward to

the wall of the hull, closing her eyes and trying to remember that day. She reached out in the dark and felt the hull wall just level with her face. *Just about here, there should be a knot in the wood.*

And her fingertips found the knot. Running her fingertips over it, she felt a smooth corner of the object. But it was deep inside and too small to grip.

She took one of her earrings out of her pocket and picked at it. She listened quietly, but heard nothing and continued prying until finally, the object came loose. She touched it all over, the small rectangle, in the blackness. She cupped it in both hands and brought it to her lips, and then put it with her earring into the deep pocket of Michael's trousers.

She backed off the shelf and jumped to the floor. *He will wake up,* she thought, *but he can't see any better than I can.* She scrambled forward, rat-like, until she bumped her head on the ladder.

It was when she had reached about halfway up that irons began clanking in his pocket. Her heart was pounding so hard she almost choked. Just before she pushed herself off the top rung, the ladder shook.

She groped forward. She didn't care that

she was bruising her palms on the rough deck. She didn't even care that she had crawled into her own vomit. At last, she banged her head again and began climbing the next ladder. With every step up she imagined his hand clamping onto her bare ankle. What if he had a shackle out ready to clamp it? Or his dagger? She was afraid to let her feet rest on the rungs and almost jumped from them if they were red hot coals.

As her head rose into the open air, her eyes fell on the iron crossbar she had set down in the moonlight. She leapt out, grabbed it and turned to find that Gregorio, was halfway out of the hatch himself.

But he had his back to her. "Come here, you," he growled. He crawled onto the deck, stood up, and bent over in a drunken stagger to take out his weapon. The side of his face was dark—he must have been injured when he fell.

He was shouting again. "Where you?" He staggered unsteadily toward the hook on the railing, looking for her. She followed him silently in her bare feet. When he did not see her, he turned back. His dagger was raised and ready to thrust.

Fima stood on her tiptoes behind him and raised the iron bar as high as she could.

Then she brought it down on his head. It made a crack, and a soft grunt came from his lips. Slowly, he went over sideways, toppling off the railing onto the beach.

Fima felt sick. What had she done? She heard the *crack* over and over. But then she said to herself, *Let this man never do to anyone else what he did to us!*

She crouched and went forward until she could peek over the railing. Gregorio was lying still, face up. *Where was Sau? Had Gregorio attacked her before he came for me? Had someone kidnapped her?* Fima started down the rope ladder. At every rung she stopped to check that Gregorio had not moved.

There was a large rock under the ladder. She was just stepping from it onto the sand, when two arms gripped her hard from behind. Fima cried out.

"You're all right! Thank God!" Sau whispered. "I couldn't warn you. When Gregorio saw the ladder he got very angry and the two of them put this rock here to climb up. The other one sat on it, waiting for him. As soon as Gregorio fell and he saw his condition, he ran off."

"Where? Who was the other one? Sebastian? Where did he go?"

"No, no, he was African. He was wearing African clothes, a long-sleeved shirt and trousers. Don't worry about him, Fima. He's gone. What about the gold piece? Did you find it?"

Fima nodded. Then, looking at her hand, Sau asked, "What is that? Are you hurt? What are you holding?"

Fima looked at her hand, surprised to see that she was still clutching the iron bar. It was dark and sticky.

It was only then that she looked at Gregorio. "I was going to hit him with it again if he tried to come back up." There was an open wound on the right side of his face. Horrified at what she had done, she threw the bar off into the mangrove and rinsed the mud and blood off her feet and arms in a pool left by the last wave.

Suddenly she felt weak and she sat on the rock. Her knees began to shake as if they were independent of her body. "Let's get out of here," said Fima. "I don't ever want to see this place again."

"You can say that again," said Sau, handing her her sandals. "On your feet. Your legs look like they can dance, but let's see if they can walk."

"How's the night going for you, boys?" said a bent man seated on a thick branch by the road as Fima and Sau, breathing hard and grunting, emerged next to him. Thinking it would be a shortcut, they had just pulled themselves up the overhang at the high-water line by climbing on the exposed roots.

"We give God thanks, Sir," said Fima in her best Michael voice, but out of breath. They checked that their caps were on straight. *He doesn't know what a favour he did us by calling us 'boys' before we had a chance to speak*, Fima thought. *I would have forgotten!*

"My walking stick fell over the cliff onto the beach by that tree with the needles over there. Would you mind getting it for me?" The man seemed to chew on tobacco while he paused. "I was lucky I did not fall over myself. I cannot walk without it."

Fima and Sau looked at each other, trying not to groan. "We would be glad to do that, sir," Fima said. They turned back toward the bay, taking the long way through the bushes this time. But when they had gone a short way around a curve and were out of sight, Sau suddenly pulled Fima into the shrub. She motioned for her to crouch down and keep quiet.

Before long the same man came past them. It was true that he was bent over as he moved. But he did not move as a bent old man who used a walking stick. He was bent so he could dash from one shadow to the next. He paused often, as if watching for someone.

Sau unwrapped the towel from around the knife and held it up and ready. Fima gave her a quizzical look.

"It's him!" Sau whispered back. "He's the other one who came with Gregorio! He's wearing the same clothes." They waited until, through the bushes, they saw him. He stood on the beach in the moonlight, watching.

Then Fima and Sau set off toward their house. Their strides were as long and strong as they could manage.

CHAPTER 20
Nine months later
For Badagry

The three-month period in the Yard for the Africans released from the *Violante* and the *Gertrudes* was coming to an end in mid-April. Sau and Jina had been informed that they would be sent to York village in the Sea District. There were men there to marry who could support them.

But the twins' enthusiasm for The Circle had not waned. Every time they went to King Jimmy market to buy ingredients for cooking in the Yard they took far longer than anyone else to come back. The reason was that they spent most of their time talking to the traders about where they had come from, and what the farm land was like there, and what grew well, and what problems they had. They became more and more convinced that their farming skills were needed in the Colony.

This farm land would be their own. They would be given tools. They would be encouraged to experiment with new crops. They had identified places where there was fertile land.

The two of them had developed a reputation. There was something captivating about the way the twins worked together. People shook their heads, smiling, after talking to them. When they talked about farming, they were very persuasive. Their eyes shone and they finished each other's sentences, and it was hard to say no to anything they wanted you to do.

Sau and Jina had convinced Michael to arrange a meeting with the assistant superintendent of the Liberated African Department. In the meeting, they explained about their experience and what they had learned since they had entered the Yard. They also listened carefully to the Department's intentions; for example, the kinds of crops, such as cotton, and palm and groundnut oils, that the government wanted to grow for export. By the time the meeting was over they had not only been given land to work themselves but had been hired as an agricultural team helping the farmers to increase their crop yields in the fertile areas of Hastings and Regent. They had jobs!

Nine months had passed since Fima had retrieved her mother's gold piece. The morning after, she had studied it. It was certainly beautiful. For being so small, it was heavy. It seemed to be gold, and it had writing on it. But why would anyone wrap it up so carefully in leather? Why was it passed down through so many generations in her family? Maybe simply because it was valuable, and one day they might need the money? But where had the fear come from? Why was there so much fear about opening it? It was all a big mystery to her.

Fima had dreaded telling Michael about their adventure in the bay. She knew he wouldn't be happy about it, and he was not. In addition, she had to agree that it was careless of them to leave his hook and ladder at the beach. But in the end, Michael was simply glad they had come home safe. "Sometimes," he conceded, "you have to do risky things to support your family or sustain its traditions." She liked that he had said that.

"But I have to ask you to think, Fima. You say you wanted to retrieve this so you could show your mother that you kept it safe.

Think about that. Are you sure you really want to show it to her? Imagine how she would feel to find out that the family tradition that she had guarded so carefully, was only a piece of shiny metal! I don't know about you, but I would be ashamed to tell her that."

After that, Fima had thrown the trinket into one of the small bags where she kept her beads and earrings. Since then she had not thought more about it.

Fima was happy living in Freetown. She had joined Michael's cooperative and when he was away on a cruiser, or on jury duty, she attended the meetings for him and carried out the purchases, distributions and sales. People teased Michael that she was more shrewd than he was at business. Michael teased her that he could tell she must be getting ready to get married because she had converted her small house into an office.

Secretly, Fima knew that she was not as self-confident as she seemed. She was afraid of carrying goods upcountry to trade for rice and palm oil. She suspected nearly every stranger of having plans to kidnap her. But so far she only travelled with Michael and she was learning from him how to be safe.

He is my mentor, she thought to herself. *Having a mentor doesn't mean you are a child. It means you're learning.*

More and more Liberated Africans were arriving in Sierra Leone, and it was a challenge to accommodate them. The colonial government had been discussing emigration plans for many months. Slavery had become illegal in British colonies, so there were many opportunities for indentured servants to work in Jamaica, Trinidad, and Demerara. The Liberated African Department insisted that every emigrant understood the terms. No one was being forced to leave. Everyone who did not like living in their new home, would be provided transport to return to Sierra Leone.

There were also Liberated Africans who wanted to emigrate to Badagry. Would it be safe? That was the question. Slavery was still going on, and nowhere would they be protected as they were in the Colony of Sierra Leone. Over the ten years he had spent in Freetown, Michael had put memories of his family in the Bight of Benin behind him. But now, Fima wanted to know them.

"If we get married here in the Colonial Church of St. George's, who will come to our wedding?" she had asked Michael back in those early days. As she began attending the church with him, she saw the answer for herself: the minister was the military chaplain, and most Sundays it was soldiers and children from the schools in the parish who sat under its polished woodwork and high vaulted ceiling. When Fima kept telling Michael that the elders in his family back home would want to be consulted about his wedding, he knew it was true.

That was how Fima and Michael found themselves on their way to the Bight of Benin, two of twenty-one Liberated Africans who were emigrating to Badagry. They looked out over Freetown as their vessel left the harbour. She looked up at him, and he put his arm around her. "This is our home now, isn't it?" he said. "Don't worry, we'll be back."

A few days after they had departed, the captain announced they would be stopping in Bonthe, on Sherbro Island, for rice to cook on the trip. Their vessel avoided the Strait. It entered the river from the northwest, and docked on the wharf at Bonthe. There in front of them was York Island where Fima had been seized.

For Fima, the place held fearful

memories. The stop was a time to stay inside, and close to Michael. From a distance, she watched the porters come up the gangway with bushel-bags of rice.

Suddenly, she jumped up and gave a shout. To Michael's amazement, she rushed toward the porters, and put out her hand in front of one of them to stop his progress.

"Toby!" she cried.

CHAPTER 21
Sherbro

The stocky man turned. He laughed aloud under his load at the sight of her face. He delivered his bag to the hold and came to meet her.

"Fima! Thank God! I can't believe my eyes! We tried so hard to find you!" Fima asked the work leader for permission to speak to him and brought him over to meet Michael.

"Tell me about Mama. Have you seen her? Where is she? And Laneh? Where is Laneh?" Toby looked for a bench, and they all sat down. He sat quiet for what seemed to Fima a long time. She met Michael's eyes, but they said nothing. Fima thought, *what terrible news does he have to tell me that he has to prepare for so long?*

But then Toby began.

When Mama Boi returned to Yagoi and found Fima gone, she and Toby had both searched for her for weeks. Finally, Mama Boi had closed the shop and returned to the village. In August, Toby had taken time off work and had gone there to visit her.

"Did you know where it was? How did you know where to go? Do you mean that she told you? She never reveals that to anyone!"

"Well, I insisted. How else could I let her know if you returned? And according to what the villagers all told me, many changes had taken place."

"No! Impossible!" Fima said, mockingly. "Things never change in Mengbinteh! The way Mama tells me about it, it always seems as if it will stay the same forever. So what did you see there? How is Mama? And Papa, and Grandma Karfua?"

"They are all well. But there is a new village chief. Let me tell you what the principle change is: the women deposed the old chief."

Fima burst out laughing, and clapped her hands. She begged him to tell them more.

"I only know what they explained to me," said Toby. "Apparently, there was always an old group up there made up of women in five different villages in the area, called The Circle."

Fima and Michael stopped smiling, and sat up straight, looking at each other. *The Circle? Which Circle? Sau's Circle?*

"When the chief was deposed," Toby said, "women from these five villages were there. The old chief locked himself inside his house. He wouldn't even talk to them. They gathered in force around it and threatened to dig it up to look for a box they said was buried there."

"The box!" Fima said to Michael. "The beautiful box Sau told us about, that Chief Monda received as payment from the slave trader when he sold the founder of the Circle. So it was in Mengbinteh where this happened! Sau didn't know which village it was!"

"Shh, Fima, let him talk. Continue, Toby," said Michael. "What happened then?"

"The women were adamant. Neither the new chief nor the old one could stop them. Finally the old chief gave in. He took them in and showed them the place where the box had been buried. He said they could dig there, he would not stop them. But he said that the chief before him had told him that the box was not there anymore, or anywhere else. It had disappeared even during the time of Chief Monda. The chief before him said that it was either the Founder's witchcraft that made it disappear, or else it was stolen by one of Chief Monda's wives.

"When he said this, the women fell silent," Toby said. "They were struck dumb. The last remaining symbol of the Circle was not only gone but it had been gone for many years, and there was no hope of finding it again.

"Watching them, the old chief felt sorry. He told them more details about the box to encourage them. He said the chief before him had told him that it was gold, and very small, and almost flat, and engraved with black writing, and rectangular."

Fima and Michael both jumped up and looked at each other, wide-eyed. "What? The gold piece is a box? It opens?" shouted Fima.

"It's a locket!" said Michael.

And they rushed to their bags. Fima had to rummage among her everyday trinkets to find where she had tossed the gold piece. Finally she discovered it.

In the light they could see that there were small hinges on one long side. In fact, somehow now the whole object had taken on a new aura in their eyes. It had a glint of old time stories, of many years passed.

"Of course!" Michael said, knocking his forehead. "How could I have been so dense? This is a tablar locket! People keep verses from the Koran in them. They hang them on chains around their necks like this." He held it up on his chest.

Then he started picking and picking at it. Finally it opened, just a crack.

"Careful!" Fima cried. "Don't let anything drop out! It might break!" She cupped her hands underneath.

Slowly, Michael pried the latch open. Inside, there lay a small, five-petaled sand-dollar fossil, no bigger than a groundnut. They both stared at it quietly, without speaking. "Thank you, Sau," Fima whispered. "If it weren't for you, I would not even know what this is."

"Michael, Grandma has always told me that Great-Grandma Fima was a chief's wife. She must have been a wife of Chief Monda! I think she stole this to carry on the tradition of the Circle. But they say she went away when Grandma Karfua was a baby. They say she gave the packet to a friend to give to her daughter, Grandma Karfua, when she got older."

"Now that I think about it, her leaving can only mean one thing," Michael said,

"Your Great-Grandma Fima must have been sold into slavery."

"Yes," said Fima. "I was thinking the same thing. And naturally, she would wrap the fossil up tightly! And of course she would tell everyone not to open it—it was too dangerous to own, if whoever was found with it would be taken captive and sold away."

"And at that time there were no Royal Navy cruisers to stop the slaver from crossing the Atlantic, so she would have been taken on to the Americas. Was Karfua her only child?"

"I don't even know. Oh, Michael, there are so many things I want to know. I want to know who the friend was who kept the bundle for Grandma Karfua until she grew up. And I want to show my mother why the bundle was so important. And I want to know if all the women in the village know the story of the Circle? And, . . ."

"Whoa, that's a lot of questions!" Michael said, laughing.

"There are more! I want to ask my mother if the reason she always told me that Mengbinteh is too dangerous for me to visit, is because people disappear from there. And is that why no one objects that the road to

Mengbinteh is so bad that no carts or wagons can go there—because they want to protect the village?"

"All right, enough questions from you. Now it's my turn. What I want is to meet your mother and your father and your grandmother so I can ask them for your hand in marriage.

"And I think if we really want replies to any of these questions, we had better take some action before those porters finish loading the rice!"

Fima threw her arms around him and kissed him. "Thank you, Michael!" she said, and rushed off to locate Toby. They hurriedly gathered up their bags and started down the gangplank that led down to the dock into Bonthe.

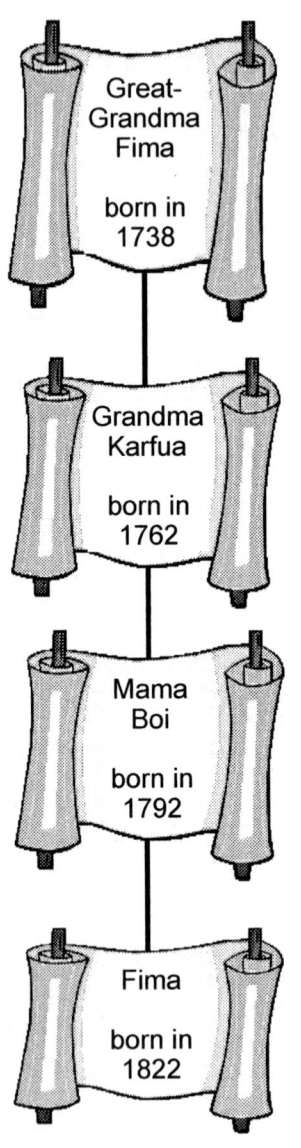

Epilogue

This book is dedicated to the many, many children who, instead of landing in the Americas as slaves, entered the Crown Colony of Sierra Leone between 1808 and 1860 as Liberated Africans because the British Royal Navy and the Mixed Commission Courts intercepted their voyages. Some had been captured by slave traders many thousands of miles away; others were captured within the area we now know as Sierra Leone, and areas in-between.

I especially dedicate it to two of these "New People" who inspired the characters in this book: a young corporal in the Militia band and a 16-year-old girl who arrived just ten days before her marriage was being arranged. All we know about them is contained in this letter written by an official in the Liberated African Department[1]:

---

[1] Harriet Tubman Resource Centre. Digital Archive. Sierra Leone Public Archive Collection, entry no. 364 in the *Liberated African Department Letter Book 1837-1842, 22nd August 1837-15th February 42*.

The text reads,

21st January 1839

Sir,

I have to request that you would have the goodness to grant a Marriage License to the undermentioned parties:

Michael Tosin, Corporal, Militia Band, Parish of St. George

Feemah alias Rebecca Thomas, a female Liberated African landed from the Portuguese Schooner "Violante" and numbered in Register 14629.

[Addressed to] Thos. Cole, Surrogate	*[Signed] W.G. Terry, Asst. Supt., Liberated African Department*

The Heritage Keeper is a work of historical fiction. I wanted to know what might have happened to bring Michael and Fima together, and what their lives might have been like.

Apart from the people, events and places which inspired the narrative, all the characters, places and plot came from my imagination. However, the facts are true: all the events could have happened in 1839 in the Colony of Sierra Leone.

The Heritage Keeper is a coming-of-age story. It is also a story of concealment and disguise. I invite the reader to make a list of all the hidden things, mistaken identities, illusions and deceptions they can find in the book to better understand the times in which the story takes place.

ACKNOWLEDGEMENTS

I am endebted to the internet for the scattered thousands of snippets of primary source material it contains about this particular place at this time in history. Any failure to find them all, and any errors in interpretation the reader may find are wholly mine! I especially want to express my appreciation of the Sierra Leone Public Archives Collection at the Harriet Tubman Resource Centre (The Harriet Tubman Institute).

I owe many thanks and much respect to my family, especially to Candace Lee, Sibyl Harleston and Simone Anderson who read the manuscript of this book and gave marvelously insightful, helpful feedback.

Most of all I thank my husband, Sam, for everything.